$3.50

TALONS

JOHN DeCHANCIE is the author of two dozen books—both fiction and non-fiction—and his novels in the fantasy and science fiction genres have been attracting a wide readership for more than fifteen years. His humorous fantasy series, beginning with *Castle Perilous*, became a bestseller for Berkley/Ace. He has also written in the horror genre, and for publications as widely varied as *Penthouse* and *Cult Movies*. His short fiction has appeared in *The Magazine of Fantasy and Science Fiction* and in numerous original anthologies, including *Castle Fantastic* (co-edited with Martin Greenberg) and his latest, *Spell Fantastic*. His most recent book, *Other States of Being* (published by Pulpless.com, Inc.), is a story collection.

TALONS

JOHN DeCHANCIE

ibooks
new york
www.ibooksinc.com

DISTRIBUTED BY SIMON & SCHUSTER, INC

An Original Publication of ibooks, inc.

Copyright ©2002 Top Cow Productions, Inc.

Witchblade®,™ & ©2001 Top Cow Productions, Inc.

An ibooks, inc. Book

Distributed by Simon & Schuster, Inc.
1230 Avenue of the Americas, New York, NY 10020

ibooks, inc.
24 West 25th Street
New York, NY 10010

The ibooks World Wide Web Site Address is:
http://www.ibooksinc.com

ISBN 0-7434-3501-X
First ibooks, inc. printing February 2002
10 9 8 7 6 5 4 3 2 1

Edited by Steven A. Roman

Special thanks to Matt Hawkins

Cover photograph of Yancy Butler by Frank Ockenfels
copyright © 2001 Turner Network Television

Cover design by Mike Rivilis & carrie monaco
Interior design by Michael Mendelsohn at MM Design 2000, Inc.

Printed in the U.S.A.

To
HARLAN ELLISON,
the better cordwainer

PROLOGUE

VIENNA, AUSTRIA, 1986

Demel's coffee-house was not crowded that afternoon. In a far corner, directly under a painting of the youthful Franz Josef, Horst Pfordmann sat sipping coffee with whipped cream, and drinking in the *Gemutlichkeit*. The German word does not translate easily: coziness, congeniality, a feeling of belonging. However one defines it, Demel's had it. It had good coffee, too.

And pastry. A table near the counter was piled with confections the like of which only Vienna could produce: vanilla crescents, Congress doughnuts, Sacher tortes, endless varieties of cookies, lady fingers, and more, most fattening in the extreme, all looking absolutely mouthwatering. But Horst wasn't hungry.

He looked around at the customers: a bespectacled old Frau writing a letter; an elderly couple in the opposite corner drinking melange—half milk, half coffee; a pretty waitress in the back on break, sipping a soda; a man in a dark suit reading a paper. Horst wondered what would any of these people do if they knew what he knew. If what fell into his lap would fall into theirs, what would

1

they do? That frump of a *gnadige Frau*, there, scribbling a newsy missive to her sister in Munich, what would she do? Who would she turn to? To whom would she divulge the secret?

Whom do you trust? Good question. Horst reached inside his jacket and fingered the padded envelope again.

In the envelope was a floppy disk, and on that disk was a file. The file had come in over an international bulletin-board network, but the accompanying e-mail note had not been coded, and the note had let on what was contained in the encrypted file. Why Dr. Pastorius had done it that way, Horst did not know. Perhaps he did not fully understand the workings of computer networks, a fairly new phenomenon. Sometimes even Horst forgot that two people communicating on net was like shouting into bullhorns on opposite sides of a crowded public square. Anything one did on a public network could be monitored by anyone in the world. Every intelligence-gathering organization on the planet routinely patrolled cyberspace for anything that might be a threat . . . or an opportunity.

But only Horst had the key to the encrypted file. It was in his pocket, on the disk with Dr. Pastorius's file. Only Pastorius could decipher Horst's files and messages. It was the same code, and it was unique. And that code could not be broken by any means known at present.

The code was, in principle, unbreakable. Neither ordinary complexity nor subtlety was its guarantee of secrecy. A thousand supercomputers working in concert for a thousand years could not unscramble the data. Of course, Horst had no guarantee that Pastorius did not send the same file, under a different encryption, to someone else. If

2

so, Pastorius had not let on. The possibility that someone else had the file comforted Horst a little, but not much.

He got up. The *gnadige Frau* smiled at him toothily as he left the coffee-house.

Walking through the elegant commercial clutter of the Kohlmarkt, Horst got a sudden urge to do something, to make a decision. He had to communicate with somebody. This thing was too big for him alone. He saw a mail kiosk, stepped up to it, took out the small padded envelope, and slipped it in the slot. He sighed. Done. Now it was out of his hands. But had he done the right thing? As he walked away from the kiosk, doubts arose. Was Pastorius simply the crank that most of his colleagues around the world thought him?

Was he crazy? Was that file and its purported secret simply a delusion? Pastorius was eccentric; was he also stark staring mad?

He wanted to forget about the whole thing. There was no way he could gain any professional recognition out of merely relaying Dr. Pastorius's findings to the proper experts.

Then there was Kenneth Irons in New York. He was an amateur, of course, but he seemed to know more about the artifact than anyone. In fact, Irons sometimes sounded as if he already was in possession of the artifact, and was simply trawling the professional field to see what others knew about it. Curious. But how could he have it? No, he was just a well-informed amateur.

Well, now I know possibly more about the ancient magical gauntlet than anyone else in the world, Horst thought.

He turned into his apartment building and mounted

the two flights to his floor. Stopping just short of the door to his flat, a mild depression came over him. The good thing about living alone was that when you came back home, your apartment was always the same way you left it. But that was also the bad thing. A loneliness welled up in him, a loneliness that had been with him throughout his adolescence and his young-adult life. He had never had a steady girlfriend. Women had never taken to him. It wasn't that Horst was bad-looking. He was just painfully shy and fearful of rejection.

He was not a virgin, and, in fact, had had a few very brief affairs. But so far he had not managed to snare a steady mistress. He was lonely most of the time.

He suddenly decided to take the underground to Rotenturmstrasse and pick up a girl.

Or perhaps . . . he'd been told of a very good place on . . . now where had Franz said it was? He checked his wallet. Not enough money. He'd have to hit an automatic teller machine. But did he have his ATM card?

No, he did not. For a second, a sinking feeling hit him as he wondered whether he might have left the plastic card in the slot the last time he used an ATM. But, no. He'd never done that; no reason he should have started.

Wait. He remembered he'd done a housecleaning job on his wallet recently, generally slimming the thing down, throwing away old business cards and dozens of slips of paper with girls' telephone numbers on them (numbers he rarely had the courage to dial). He hated a bloated wallet; rather, one bloated with anything other than money. He might have left the ATM card in his desk drawer. Well, he'd have to go into the flat after all.

He got out his key and opened the door, and walked into darkness. And stopped. He distinctly recalled leaving

4

a light on. Bulb must have blown out. As he edged cautiously toward the alcove that stood for his study, a curious feeling came over him, one he couldn't readily identify. Something was not right. He flicked on the light, and saw what was wrong. Two men were standing in opposite corners of the alcove.

They stepped forward. One was taller, and wore a black trench coat over a brown suit. The other had on an expensive-looking black leather jacket over a blue turtleneck. He had an ugly face but a pleasant manner.

"You're probably wondering," the toad-like man said in a Prussian accent, "who the hell we are and what we're doing here." He smiled.

Horst had frozen. His only thought was *police*. He could only stutter, "Who . . . who . . . ?"

"Relax," said the taller one. He was fairly good-looking, with dark eyes and a wide mouth. "First of all, you are Horst Pfordmann?"

Horst nodded.

"Graduate student, University of Vienna. Archaeology?"

Horst nodded again.

"Good, at least we have the right man. We're interested in the Witchblade code."

"The . . . the Witchblade—"

"I said relax," the man told him mildly. "Nothing's going to happen to you if you cooperate. Recently you received data from a Dr. Helmut Pastorius in Egypt, concerning the Witchblade. It was encrypted. We need the de-encryption code."

Horst finally drew himself together. "Who the hell are you?"

"Who do you think?" the taller man said, shrugging.

He had a symmetrical face with movie-star good looks that Horst knew women really went for.

"It's private information," Horst said, trying not to sound as frightened to the core as he was.

"Not any more. We need this data for our case files."

"Who are you?" Horst demanded. "What branch of the government?"

"My name is Erwin Strauss," said the toad. "We need the code. If we have to, we'll impound your computer and every floppy disk you have."

"I want to see some identification. I don't think either of you are Austrian."

"You won't give it up?"

"I must refuse. You have no right . . . no . . ."

Strauss reached into his jacket and drew out a .9mm pistol with a silencer.

Horst saw his death coming, and in the few seconds of his life remaining, as the numbed shock of realization paralyzed him, his only thought, a wild shouting in his mind, was that it could not possibly end this way, so quickly, with so little warning. Things like this did not happen. There was no way it could happen to him. Not to him. Not like this.

The small apartment resounded with a dull thud. Horst Pfordmann fell backward to the tile floor, a single, oozing hole in his forehead. The two intruders cocked their ears for any reaction outside the apartment.

When nothing seemed forthcoming, the taller man sighed. "Nice shot, Strauss. Though I wish . . ."

Strauss put the pistol-with-silencer back in his shoulder holster. He scowled. "It's better, cleaner, this way. You have any objection?"

6

"Forget it. It's just that the last time I was in Vienna, I got shot."

"I remember. You took a bullet in the chest. You didn't die."

"I lead a charmed life."

"Let's gather up this stuff."

The men made short work of it. In minutes they had cleared the apartment of every floppy disk, in all formats, that could be found in drawers and file cabinets, on shelves, and on the desk. In doing so, they methodically trashed the room, artfully littering the floor and misarranging furniture to make it look as though the place had been burgled. They accomplished these tasks making as little sound as possible.

"Get his wallet and his watch," the tall one ordered. Strauss obeyed.

"Telephone-address book?"

"Probably on his hard disk," Strauss replied.

"Check anyway."

"Right." As the ugly one rummaged through the desk, his leather-jacketed colleague dumped all the floppies into a plastic shopping bag.

"Got it," Strauss said after a few moments. "Telephone-address book. Let me plant the cocaine, and we'll leave."

"Does it need that?"

"Can't hurt. Drug deal goes bad, man's dead."

Strauss took out a small plastic bag filled with a white substance and lightly powdered the desk top with it. After sprinkling some on the floor, he folded up the bag again and pocketed it. "That ought to do it. Just traces."

The trenchcoated one stripped the computer's Central

Processing Unit of its peripheral components: keyboard, printer, mouse, external modem, joystick. He unplugged the power cord, and after hefting the CPU, he picked it up. "We just walk out, right? No guilty looks, like we own the place."

"Like we're repossessing a computer."

The thin mouth over the strong jaw turned upward wryly. "No one repossesses a damned computer. Practically no resale value."

"All right, you're the computer expert."

"Here we are in the age of science and technology, and we're running around chasing after ancient talismans."

"I wonder how long we'll have jobs at all, after *glasnost*," Strauss muttered. He groaned as the computer shifted in his arms. "This bastard is heavy."

The two men left the apartment. The tall one shut the door gently. It locked automatically

No one noticed them, much less challenged them, as they left the building.

CHAPTER
ONE

Sara Pezzini came running around the corner of the alley and saw that the man she was chasing, a crackhead snitch who called himself "Kool Whip," was far ahead. It was dark in the shadows behind these old warehouses, dirty-bricked old hulks that would probably be luxury apartments one day.

I only wanted to ask you a few questions, is what she wanted to yell to the guy, but it sounded lame even to her. She'd no sooner got out of the plain-brown-wrapper police car than he'd bolted, athletic shoes chirping *squeak squeak squeak* against wet concrete. He was a streak before she got up to speed. The guy could run.

As she followed, the strange bracelet on her left wrist began to throb. Just faintly, just edging over the threshold of tactile sensation.

Faintly or not, the bracelet didn't throb often.

It was drizzling in New York. The sky was slate gray. It had been drizzling all day without ever adding up to real rain. Nevertheless, puddles had accumulated in gouges, potholes, and cracks, lay oily and glistening in plugged

9

drains and odd depressions. Sara's sneakered foot splashed into a deep one.

"Damn it."

Then her *squish-slap squish-slap* went chasing after Kool Whip's annoying squeak. This operation was already turning into a Keystone Cops scenario. It wasn't much of an operation anyway, just routine questioning of an informer who was in the habit of supplying valuable info now and then, if it could be scared out of him. He was scared now, that was sure, but of what? He'd run at the very sight of Sara, and that could mean only one thing: Kool Whip was good for the clubbing death of a junkie down near East 29th Street and First Avenue last night.

He hadn't even been on Sara's list of usual suspects. Whip was not the violent type, but he was a little hot headed, and anyone can get riled enough at someone to pick up a length of two-by-four and cave in a skull. Now and then.

Slap-squish slap-squish . . .

Squeak squeak squeak . . .

That wet shoe was really vexing. And it was soaked, too, down to the sock.

An incongruous thought flashed: she wondered if she had a dry pair in her desk drawer somewhere. No, why should she? Wait, in her locker. Didn't she once come into work with a change of clothes to play racquetball, and wasn't that last week? No, two . . . three weeks ago.

Don't worry about the damn sock. Catch the suspect.

"Whip, wait up!"

Tearing around another corner, Whip didn't answer

"I just wanna ask—" She slowed, more disgusted than winded. She'd been slow to react.

Now he was lost in shadow. Gone.

Her cell phone tweeted.

"Rats." She stopped and took it off the hook on her belt and hissed an exasperated "Yes?"

"Well, excuse me all to hell."

"Jake?"

"Right. Your partner. Your bosom buddy."

"I'm the one with the bosom, buddy."

"Don't think I'm not aware."

"Sometimes I wonder if you're conscious half the time. Whassup? How's your flu?"

"It's not the blue kind," Jake McCarthy said. "I'm really sick."

"So am I."

"What, you catch it, too?"

"No, sick of chasing geeks through back alleys."

"Who're you chasing now?"

"I was. Kool Whip, a.k.a. Charles Morton Bromley, the Second."

"Are you kidding me? That's his real name?"

"I just looked at his file. He comes from a well-to-do Boston family."

"Get out."

"Nope."

"You lose him?" Jake asked.

"Yup."

"Excellent work, Detective Pezzini."

"Up yours. He ducked into a door. I'll find him."

"Call backup."

"I can handle it."

Jake coughed away from the phone.

"Hello?" Sara said.

"Sorry. Yeah, I think you can. You think he brained Smokey?"

11

"Why did he run?" Sara wanted to know.

" 'Urban anxiety' or whatever they call it. He's afraid of cops, the poor little tyke."

"They hung out a lot. We know they sometimes didn't get along. Whip has a short fuse. Ergo . . ."

"Ergo. One question, though. Why's he so stupid as to run?"

"Whip can't think straight when he's strung out."

"Okay, Pez," Jake said. "I'll go along with it. Wish I was there."

"No, you don't. Get rid of that bug. Wait a minute. Why did you call?"

"Seltzer phoned me about you. He's not what you call favorably disposed toward you, Pez."

"What other revelations do you have for me today?"

"Says you haven't returned his calls."

"I never return his calls."

"I know, and he knows. I guess he called the chief and asked about you, and the chief said to talk to her partner."

"What'd he want from you?"

"Asked if you had any friends in organized crime."

"He asked you that?"

"Yeah."

"Why the hell?"

"Dunno, Pez. I think he's got a new theory about you."

"What do you think it is?"

"That you're mobbed up in some way."

"Of all the . . . He actually said this?"

"Not in so many words, but that's what the whole conversation was noodling towards."

"He's crazy."

"He's Internal Affairs. They're all paranoid up there."

"Maybe I'll drop by your place today," Sara said.

"Don't. You'll get this crud I got."

"You California boys shouldn't ever come east. You belong on Zuma Beach getting a tan and hanging ten."

"Or hanging with surfer girls. I do miss the beach. Nothing like roasting marshmallows on a driftwood fire at night."

"Catch you later. I have to roast one of our East Side snitches. On a spit, if possible."

Sara flipped the phone shut and rehooked it.

Now, where the hell did Whip get to? Ah, a gouged and battered steel fire door hanging open, service entrance to a large abandoned building. She took out a small, slim but quite powerful lithium ion flashlight from her back pocket.

Beyond the doorway lay jumbled shapes in the darkness: hulks of dead machinery, piles of boxes, assorted junked equipment all over a debris-littered floor. Everything of worth had been stripped away. Pipes had been cut, plumbing fixtures removed, even some windows had been surgically excised, carried away and sold long ago. After some cleanup, the structure would be ready for gutting and renovation. On her salary, Sara wouldn't be able to afford the condos and apartments that would result.

Sara tiptoed through a vast ruined silence, listening. Coming to a stairwell, she looked up, playing the tight, focused beam of the light through creepy shadows. She didn't like the prospect of going up those stairs. Whip wasn't ordinarily dangerous, but he scared easily. And frightened little men are to be treated circumspectly, she had discovered in her career as a detective for the Police Department of the City of New York.

She turned off her cell phone and listened. The building

creaked and moaned. Sara cocked her head to one side. Maybe he didn't duck in here. But out in the alley his squeaking had stopped at about where the door was.

She began to tour the ground floor of the building, following a corridor lined with more debris, wreck, and ruin. Every door she came across was nailed shut from the inside.

She called out, "Whip! Come on, dude. I just want to ask you something."

Silence.

"Just a talk. That's all I want."

Nothing.

"I'm not taking you in."

Lie. She had to haul him in now.

She went on, "There's just a few things I need to know."

More creaking upstairs.

"Shit," she said to herself.

She turned to walk away. Maybe he got out some way. Well, she wasn't going to risk stumbling around in this wreckage.

"I got nothing for you!"

She stopped and whirled, then walked cautiously through an archway into an expansive open area surrounded by a tier of railed balconies. What kind of place was this? There were things here, hulking in the darkness. Strange-looking things. "Whip, that you?"

"Yeah. I don't have anything for you today, Pez." The voice echoed hollowly, coming from one of the galleries above the huge open space. She played the beam upward but couldn't see its source.

"I haven't asked you anything yet," she said.

"You wanna know about Smokey."

"Okay."

"I heard he was killed. He tended to piss people off. Someone got mad at him and hit him."

"Did you do it?"

"No. He was my friend."

"You two mixed it up a couple of times."

"Sure, we had a tiff now and then. But I swear, Pez. I didn't hit him over the head."

"How do you know how he was killed?"

"I heard."

"You hear a lot."

"That's what you always say. That's why you hassle me all the time."

"How many times have I hassled you this year?"

"Uh . . ."

"Come on," Sara wanted to know. "How often did I ask you for information on a case I was working on? This past year."

"Who keeps track?"

"Once, Whip. Once this year. I checked. I just looked at your file. Now, is that all the time?"

"How do I know how often you bother the shit out of me? It seems like all the time."

"Accuracy in media. Come on down, Whip."

What the hell was this stuff down on the floor? Jumbles of metal in odd configurations: grates and lattices, geometrical arrangements, juxtapositions and structures. It looked like . . .

"I didn't do anything."

"Why did you run?"

"I didn't run," Whip said.

"You walk faster than anyone I've ever seen."

"I saw you parking the car and I just had somewhere to go, so I went."

Sara had never noticed the Boston accent before. *Pahking the cahh* . . . It wasn't thick, just a trace, but it was there. Amazing what you don't pick up. "You were a little too quick. I gotta ask you about Smokey."

"So ask."

"When was the last time you saw him?"

"Christ, I don't know."

"When was it?"

"Don't know. Couple of days ago."

"Where?"

"How do I know where? On the street."

"When?"

"Two days ago."

"How about last night?"

"Didn't see him."

"Where didn't you see him?"

"On the street."

This was getting nowhere. Besides, she was distracted. *Sculpture.* Suddenly she knew what she was looking at. She walked past an odd assortment of tall conical, wickedly pointed shapes. Metal sculpture. Some artist was squatting here, using the place for a studio. The stuff looked pretty good. She was no judge but thought she saw talent sitting in the blackness.

Back to business.

"Whip, get your ass down here or I'm coming up to get you."

"Stay away from me."

Whip started moving as Sara walked back through the archway and went to the stairwell, which she mounted, taking each littered step carefully and letting the flash beam lance the darkness ahead. It looked clear to the second level. She came forth onto a wide balcony strewn with mountings for missing machinery. Apparently the artist's squatting rights didn't extend beyond the ground floor. This had been some kind of shop, probably a metal shop. Maybe the artist had worked here at some point, then came back to make art. She gave a glance downward, where the sculptures brooded in shadow. This guy—or gal, for that matter—could have quite a show.

"Where are you?" Sara demanded.

He stood by the rail running along the balcony. "Keep away, I'm warning you."

"Stay cool, dude. Nothing's going to happen." *Except now I gotta arrest you*, Sara thought.

Whip was telepathic, apparently. "You're not going to bust me," Whip said. "You can't. You don't have a warrant."

"Don't need one if you flee an interview. That means I get to take you in for questioning. You'd played it cool . . ."

"I'm telling you, I didn't run."

"Look, if you give up the truth about what happened, it could be Man One instead of murder. It could be something even less."

"I didn't kill him!"

Edge of desperation now, a cornered quavering to the voice that kept retreating as Whip bumped into things and sent debris skittering across the floor.

"Okay, so let's talk about it," Sara said in her best touchy-feely voice. "Smokey stole from you again, right? He took your money when you were sleeping. He needed a fix, he ripped you off. He'd done it before and you got mad, madder than ever before. So you picked up . . . what was it? What did you hit him with, Whip?"

"I didn't. Stay away from me, you."

"You stay right where you are."

He didn't, then suddenly began climbing, and Sara's sweep of light picked up a rickety ladder running between levels. Sara heard him clamber to the next balcony. She reentered her stairwell and went up another flight.

"Tell me what happened, Whip."

"Nothing happened. I haven't seen him in weeks."

"I thought you said you saw him a few days ago."

"Keep away."

Sara stopped. "Whip, I've never seen you like this. Listen, it's not so bad. You have a family, don't you? Your parents are well-off. They can help you. They can get you a good lawyer."

"*Stay away from me!*"

Sara stopped, letting the panicked echoes die. He was freaking out. Withdrawal symptoms? Probably. Smokey had stolen all his ready cash, and that was a tough position for an addict like Whip to be in.

"What's wrong?" she asked.

"You."

"What's wrong with me?"

"You kill guys all the time."

"What?"

"I know about you. You don't like someone, you think they're dirty, they've done something, you take 'em out. Guys get dead around you a lot, lady."

"It's not true." She winced saying it.

"You're some kind of witch. That's what I hear."

"Who says this crap?"

"Lots of people. You're a killer cop. You're a . . . I don't know what. You're a monster."

"Cut it out. Kool Whip, I gotta take you in. We have to talk, and you have to come clean. It'll be better all around. You can call your family."

Whip laughed maniacally. "You have no idea what you're saying."

"You don't talk to them?"

"They don't talk to me. They talk only to Lowells and Cabots, and maybe God once in a while, when they have time for him."

"You don't get along?"

"I haven't seen them in ten years. Not since I dropped out of Columbia."

"Well, maybe it's time for a reconciliation. But, look, this has nothing to do with Smokey's death. Just tell me where you were last night. That's all I want to know."

"Get away from me, Pezzini!" He was screeching now.

"Whip, calm down."

There was no more room for retreat. He suddenly turned and leapt upward. Balancing on the thin railing, he put one foot on a rung of the ladder.

The ladder suddenly collapsed under his weight, and he fell.

"Whip!"

There was no sound but metal clattering to the floor. But with it came a strange, muted sound, like a knife going into an overripe melon.

Sara came to the edge of the balcony and sent the flash beam down, trying to make sense of what she saw.

19

He had fallen on one of the sculptures. The beam illuminated his face, which bore a look of such shock and dismay that it made Sara's stomach lurch.

She rushed down the stairwell, came out onto the floor, and advanced toward Whip's still moving body.

He had landed on a metal spike. The man was impaled, skewered like so much meat, a huge spear of metal running up through his bowels.

She couldn't look. There was nothing to do for him. No 911 call would save him, though she got out her phone and punched in the numbers anyway as he made muted, gurgling noises deep in his throat and twitched horribly.

Mercifully, he didn't do either for long.

After she got off the phone she saw what the artist had spray-painted on one of the other sculptures:

USELESS JUNK

It wasn't a gang tag, not a graffiti vandal's comment. It was artfully done, a despairing wail of self doubt from the sculptor himself. He had given up, abandoned his squatter studio and its contents. His life's work, perhaps.

HOPELESS

The Witchblade made a dull drumbeat against her wrist.

CHAPTER

TWO

She stood in the alley, watching the paramedics take the body out on a gurney. It had taken them a long time, an agonizingly long, horrid time, to get him off the sculpture. He'd died before they arrived, she guessed, but only the autopsy would make that clear.

The Witchblade was quiet now. She wondered what it had been trying to tell her, if anything. It had seemed mildly interested in the death of Charles Morton Bromley, the Second. As if it might be of some significance, but only in the abstract.

Footsteps up the alley.

"Pezzini!"

She turned. It was her boss, Captain Joe Siry.

Siry walked straight up to her and brought his haggard face up close to hers, close enough so that she smelled his sour breath. She wasn't particularly keen on monitoring his oral health.

"You have an explanation?" he demanded.

"Simple."

He backed up a little. "Well, now, if it's so simple, why don't you tell me."

"Okay," she said with a shrug. "Nothing special."

"Not what I heard. I heard you got a guy run through like a shish-kabob in there."

"That's not a particularly tasteful way of putting it, but, yeah. There was a freak accident as the result of the suspect's resisting arrest."

"This was a suspect?"

"Not exactly. He was an informant."

"And you were arresting him?"

"I tried to question him on a routine investigation. He ran. He had an accident. Fell and got impaled on some metal sculpture."

Siry turned at looked at the building. "Metal sculpture. This an art gallery?"

"In a way. Place is full of somebody's sculpture. Abandoned looks like."

"What makes you say that?"

"Some indications. You'll get the report."

"So this guy wasn't even a perp. He wasn't a suspect at all."

"Not until he ran, Joe. Then it was pretty obvious . . ."

"What was obvious?"

"That he was good for the killing."

"Nothing's ever obvious. You have any proof?"

"Not a lot."

Siry began pacing. "Fingerprints?"

"No murder weapon yet."

"Christ."

"What's up?" Sara asked.

"We have an evaluation coming up. I'm trying to think of how to play this."

"What's there to play?"

"To quote you, not a lot."

"It was an accident, Joe."

He poked a finger at her. "That's 'Captain Siry' to you, Detective."

"Okay. A freak accident. That's all."

"Too many," Siry grumbled, still pacing.

"Too many what?"

"Too many freaky things happen to you."

"So I've been told."

He stopped and he fixed her in an admonitory stare. "Don't get smart with me."

"Sorry."

That vein was popping out on his forehead again. She always had trouble stifling a laugh. She looked away.

Siry was about to add something, but footsteps brought him around to look.

"Oh, Christ."

It was Seltzer, from Internal Affairs, trooping up the alley.

"Don't answer any questions now, Pezzini," Siry told her. "Write that report, and let me see it first before you send it to him."

"I always do, Cap."

"Good evening," Seltzer said as he approached.

"Any reason for this honor?" Siry wanted to know.

Seltzer's face could be described as pleasantly mean-spirited. It was pinched and narrow and smilingly thin-lipped.

"Only the honor of watching our department's men . . . uh, personnel . . . in action."

"What's up?"

"Heard there was a death of a suspect. Have to investigate."

"Really? Even if it was an accident? Even if our man . . . if she never laid a hand on him?"

"I can't judge before I know the facts. This is just routine on my part. I'd like to see where it happened."

"In there," Sara said, pointing.

"Sounds very unusual," Seltzer said, "the circumstances." He licked his lips. "Freakish."

"It was," Sara said.

"An impaling. Is that true?"

"You make it sound like an execution."

"Was it?" Seltzer said with a leer.

"It was an accident."

"Keep quiet," Siry told her. "Let me handle this." He rotated to Seltzer. "Does she have to answer questions right this very minute? If you're going to make a full investigation, she has certain rights, okay?"

"Captain, I'm perfectly aware of departmental procedure."

"Well, maybe you're not aware of this. I'd like to think that at least the dust can settle before you begin to make accusations against one of my best—"

"I haven't made any accusations."

"Well, what the hell was it I just heard?"

Sara walked away as her boss continued sparring. Two uniformed patrolmen strolled by.

"Right up the old kazoo," one of them said with a shudder.

"Man, what a way to go," the other said.

She shivered. The fool, running like that. If he'd simply played it cool, she never would have thought him a suspect.

Routine investigation. Routine murder. Victim less than nobody. What did it matter?

But, God, what a way to die. And for nothing.

What the hell was the Witchblade's interest?

The mind of Kenneth Irons was a vast and labyrinthine place. Thoughts raced through it in geometric patterns, crossing and recrossing. Behind him, the city was a panorama of power, light-studded shafts thrusting into a black sky.

He swiveled the chair slightly. His hands formed a pyramid on his chest, fingertips almost touching his chin. His eyes swept over the things on his desk. He had kept the same accoutrements over the years. That crystal paperweight, this clock. Knick-knacks here and there. Marble-based pen set. Gold cigarette lighter. Same objects. Same desk. Many, many years. They reassured him.

He was not easily reassured.

The door to his office cracked light.

"Mr. Kontra, sir," said a voice.

"Have him come in," Irons said.

Lazlo V. Kontra entered. He nodded and sat down.

"Excuse the dim light, Mr. Kontra," Irons said. "I find it necessary to rest my eyes now and then. Shall I turn on . . . ?"

"Don't trouble yourself," Kontra said. He eased his massive frame into a leather chair. He seemed comfortable. Perhaps a little self-satisfied. His face had a certain rugged symmetry. Women found him attractive, and he knew it.

Irons regarded him. One rock cliff regarding another.

"We can do business."

Kontra nodded. "I think so."

"Computer business."

Kontra kept nodding. "One of my businesses."

"You have the foreign contacts," Irons said.

Kontra grinned. "You have financing to run big operations." His accent was thick but comprehensible. "Big."

"Yes. You can increase your staff, buy capital equipment."

"More computers. Everything today is computers."

"Indeed. Little bits of data flowing through the latticework of a massive grid. Pulses of light, throbs of electric charge. Instead of the jingle of gold we have the clicking of a hard drive. Registering dollar signs all over the globe."

"And what you do, you control the little bits," Kontra said, "You herd them like sheep, this way, that way, until they come into your barn."

Irons smiled. "Yes."

"This is new way of doing business. Forget profit."

"Rather tiresome thing to worry about, profit. The money left over after doing business. Why not just rake in the money and forget the business?"

"I like that," Kontra said.

"So do I." Irons's chair drifted to the left. "Increasingly, too many stumbling blocks in the way of making money. Too many leaks in the bucket. It's almost not worth conducting business any more. Why not herd those bleating dollars? There are flocks of them. Swarms. Trillions out in the electronic pastures. What does a few billion of them matter? Who will even notice they are gone?"

"Ah. It is even better. You don't even have to steal."

Irons chuckled. "I know. One can even indulge in the creation of money itself, *ex nihilo.*"

"Eh?"

"From nothing."

"I see. Yes."

"Like God touching his finger to the center of the void. I've done it for years. I own banks. Banks can create money, within certain governmental limits. But the new ways are even easier and can yield a lot more."

"No limits."

"Right, Mr. Kontra. No limits. And as long as your . . . uh, experts . . . stay in—where are they again?"

"Just say eastern Europe," Lazlo Kontra said. "There they are immune from arrest."

"Arrest?"

An awkward silence fell.

Kontra sat and waited.

"Whatever would they be doing that they should fear arrest?" Irons wanted to know.

"Not a thing," Kontra said. "I still need people here. I have people."

"I understand the need for monitoring your employees. Difficult to maintain control long distance. What sorts of operations have you in this country?"

Kontra shrugged. "I have lots of businesses. Moving vans. Dry cleaning. Home heating oil."

"I mean the computer experts."

"They mainly develop software."

Iron raised his eyebrows.

Kontra's smile widened. "They study firewalls."

"Yes."

"And other things," Kontra said.

"Firewalls," Irons said. "I love these metaphors."

"They describe precisely."

"Why do you keep your R&D here in the States?"

Kontra shrugged. "More experience in software development here."

"Yes, the U.S. leads."

Kontra guffawed. "You always did. I'll tell you a joke."

"Do."

"Old Soviet joke."

"You're not Russian."

"I lived in Moscow for years."

"However, your name . . . ?"

"Romanian."

"Ah."

"I'll tell you this joke. Two guys meet in Moscow airport. One is pushing huge dolly across terminal, loaded with suitcases. The other says 'Hello, Ivan, how are you doing?' Ivan says. 'I've been developing Soviet People's Pocket Computer.' The guy says, 'We have a pocket computer? Ours?' Ivan says, 'Yes, it's ours. We didn't steal it from West.' He takes small computer out from pocket. The guy looks at it. Has nice screen, easy keyboard. The guy says, 'That's marvelous! I can't believe we did this.' Ivan says, 'I got to go.' He starts pushing. The guy says, 'What's all this?' Ivan says, 'Oh, that is power supply.' "

Irons's sudden laughter was genuine. His face cracked like a limestone palisade. "Hadn't heard that one."

"Funny, eh?"

"Very. You worked for Russian intelligence for years. Before you defected."

"First was with Romanian military intel, then went to civilian intel, and then to KGB in Soviet Union. I was with them long time."

28

"But you obviously had extracurricular activities."

"Yes. I did lots of things *na levo*. On the left hand. Underground. Black market. Only way you could make enough money to live well. Whole country was *na levo*, or you starve."

"Then you came to New York."

"I defect in New York. I like it. I stayed."

"Still a great city, despite recent tragedies."

"Yes. So, we can do business."

"I think so, Mr. Kontra." Irons's smile glowed in the shadows.

"Good," Kontra said.

"You will hear from me soon. Through intermediaries. Does that suit you, Mr. Kontra?"

"Certainly, Mr. Irons."

"It's been a pleasure."

Kontra rose and left the room.

Irons contemplated the silence for a moment. Then he got up and went to the window. He looked out on the city. Oblongs of light speckled a forest of tall shapes. Below, white lights approached, red lights receded. Glowing like a stormy sea, low clouds touched the tops of the highest buildings. At night the city seemed insubstantial and mysterious. The realm of another world.

His thoughts were not on business. They were on the Witchblade.

THREE

It was late when Kontra got back to Brooklyn and home. The apartment building was quiet. The murmurs of televisions and radios were muffled—insistent voices, barely heard, chattering away on the other side of the walls, as if the building's roaches had gathered for a political rally.

The hall smelled. The hall always smelled, though it wasn't a bad one. Faint odors of cabbage. Maybe it wasn't cabbage. *Somebody* had cabbage, he decided. It was one of those bad-good smells, cabbage. He had eaten enough of it. He liked it, in fact. But it was not so good in a hall. People should use their kitchen exhaust fans. He was used to odors in hallways. Even now, when he could afford it, he did not buy a single-family dwelling. In this city they were horrifically expensive, but he could have one if he wanted it. That wasn't the issue. Apartment living was habit, what he was used to.

His stalwart bulk mounted the stairs. He didn't like elevators. He remembered living in a six-floor walkup when he had a low post in the army.

He was big. There was some middle-age ballast on

30

him, but it covered a spring-steel mass of muscle. He was built like a stout tree, and his arms were long and thick. His legs were a little short, but that made him even more powerful.

Quiet. He stopped to listen. The late evening news? No, it was well after eleven. *The Tonight Show*? He wanted to sit and look at the *Tonight Show*. He moved up the stairs.

Ah, the sound was coming from his apartment. His wife was up watching the television. He fumbled in his pocket for his keys. The *tuica*, plum brandy, was a little sour in his stomach tonight. He wondered if there were any antacid in the bathroom cabinet.

"Good night."

A voice to his right, a visitor coming out of the neighbor's. He glanced, and the face was familiar. Ever so faintly . . .

Where was that door key? He wasn't drunk, but he had downed a few glasses. Just a few.

That man. He turned to look again. The man was aiming a silenced compact semiautomatic.

At him.

"What?" was all Kontra could say. Then a thought occurred: *Shit! The neighbors are in Europe.*

The pistol snapped once. He felt a poke in the chest, as if a buddy had landed a good punch on him.

The guy was trying to kill him! The rotten, no good . . . *"Bastard!"*

The gun went off again. Enraged, Kontra rushed the hit man, who by now had a puzzled look.

"God damn you!" Kontra roared as he lunged.

The man panicked and raised the pistol for a head shot. But he never got it off, for Kontra had the gun in both hands, twisting it upward. He had moved like a striking snake, like a demented bear. The gun fired again into the ceiling, then went flying off, bounced against wallpaper, and fell to the carpet.

Kontra had the guy trapped in the blind hallway, hands around his neck. He squeezed. He had always liked the feeling of a human neck in his hands. He could feel the arteries closing, feel the soft muscles collapse. Nothing could break Kontra's hold. No one ever had, for all that they beat and flailed and tried to come up between his arms. No routine judo countermove could work. Kontra was too strong.

He did it as he had done it to prisoners. The technique was to strangle them until they passed out, then slap them back to life. They did not expect to wake up again, and when they did, they were cooperative. It made interrogation a lot simpler. True, a few had never revived. But not many.

He would streamline the technique now. He squeezed and squeezed. The terrified man's face turned red, then changed to a dark shade of purple-green. He kicked at Kontra's shin. Kontra ignored it.

There was a bell ringing somewhere. He couldn't figure why a bell was ringing. Like a chime. He ignored it and kept up the pressure on the man's neck.

But damn that bell. Then he noticed that he couldn't see much. Everything in his peripheral vision was black. Only the man's discolored face was visible.

And then he realized that he was losing consciousness, and that, as bull-strong as he was, there was nothing he could do about it.

Sara lay almost naked on her bed. She was exhausted, and she hadn't done a thing all day. It was night. The apartment was dark.

She sat up on the edge of the bed. Then she rose and went to a television on an entertainment center on the far wall.

She halted as she moved to turn it on; instead, she switched on the compact disc player. The tiny red light seemed like a distant star. She ran a finger over the few CDs she had. No. The red star winked out.

Moving to the kitchen space, she opened the refrigerator: a lemon, a quart carton of milk, two bottles of water, and a long-forgotten Chinese take-out box. Shifting her attentions to the freezer compartment, she found a frozen diet dinner, low-fat fettuccine with clam sauce. A plastic tub of fake butter, filled presumably with leftovers she had frozen, sat beside the fettuccine.

She contemplated the contents of the compartment in a Zen fashion, then closed the freezer door.

Maybe she wasn't hungry after all.

No, she was, but she wasn't going to eat the frozen glop, and that Chinese had surely gone bad. And she couldn't for the life of her remember what was in the plastic tub. Go out?

Alone?

She sighed. "Wouldn't be the first time . . ."

The phone rang, and she crossed to it almost gratefully. "Yeah?"

"Sara?"

"Jake."

"Uh-huh. You okay?"

"Sure."

"You sound glum," Jake commented.

"I'm fine. Have you eaten?"

"Uh, kinda."

"Kinda?"

"Why, you wanted to go out?"

"Not really. I was thinking about it, but I'm too tired."

"I could use some coffee. And some cannoli. Want to meet me at Chez Nunzio?"

"Sounds good. Are you sure you're well enough?"

"I'm over it. It was a mild flu. Just starting to get my appetite back."

"Okay. Meet you in, say, half an hour?"

"Give me an hour, Sara."

"Okay. See you."

She put on a skirt, black and short. To hell with that. She tried her plaid one. Nope. Putting off the lower-body decision, she tried on some blouses. She had three that were nominally passable. All looked hopelessly wrinkled, hopelessly drab. God, when was the last time she ironed?

She ended up putting on jeans, black T-shirt, leather jacket. Gun. No purse. Badge. No bra.

She regarded her image in the mirror.

Let's face it, I'm butch.

She looked at her nightstand, on which the Witchblade sat. The stone seemed to glow.

Voices, tiny, distant voices babbled inside it. Or just behind it? Somewhere associated with it.

She picked it up and put it on her wrist. In this world, in its passive state, the artifact was a simple gold wire bracelet set with a puce stone. What it was in its natural habitat, nowhere in the known universe, no one knew. It was a strange manifestation, whatever the hell it was.

It was the Witchblade.

Should she wear it or not? The question always came up when she dressed to go out for a purely social occasion.

And this *was* purely social. It was her day off, and Jake was still officially out sick.

It was still on her wrist as she left the apartment.

Hospital rooms always have harsh florescent light. It shone right in his eyes. Wires and tubes connected him to various mechanisms behind him and at either hand.

Kontra looked around. Lots of machinery. Some of them beeped. Some winked lights at him. Others leaked fluids into his body. There was an oxygen hose.

He hated hospitals. But this was surely one, and he was here.

He remembered being shot at, but that was all he remembered. He had tried to do something about it. Run? No, he hadn't run. The memory was a blur. How long ago had he been shot? Yesterday? Two days ago?

Life had been a jumble since: Lights blinding him, the faces of nurses orbiting, doctors speaking, things beeping and humming. Needles jabbing in his skin. All a blur, a smear of memory.

"Hello, Mr. Kontra."

This was another doctor, he believed. Different from the one who had spoken before. At least he thought. This one looked a little older. The first one had been a baby.

"Yes."

"You're a lucky man."

"I'm going to live?"

"Yes, sir. You took two bullets to the chest. Fortunately, one of them only nicked an artery. The other collapsed a lung. You're very lucky to be alive."

"So I'll live." It was a statement.

"We still have some work to do in there. We got out both bullets, but we found something very strange."

"Strange."

"Yes. The bullets we took out were .32 caliber. They hadn't deformed much. But we found a third bullet. At least we saw it in the X-rays."

"Yes?"

"One that's been in your body quite a while. We can tell this by the tissue that's grown around it. It wasn't fired from the same gun that was used on you yesterday. It's an .8mm slug."

"Ah. Yes."

"You've been shot before?"

"Yes. Long time ago."

"Remarkable. You must have the constitution of a bull elephant."

He shrugged, and it hurt.

"Well," the doctor went on, "we couldn't get at it while we were extracting the others. We should go back in at some point and remove it."

Kontra shook his head. "It's been in twenty years. It can stay."

"Not a good idea to leave it in, Mr. Kontra."

"I will think about it."

"We won't be able to do further surgery until you've completely recovered, of course. But let's talk about it. I think we can release you in about a week and a half. Perhaps a little less, if everything stays stable. You're doing fine, actually. Remarkable. As I said . . ."

Kontra nodded. "Lucky."

"Um . . . the police would like to come in now and question you."

"Send my wife in first."

"Of course. I'm sure they'll understand."

"The man, he got away?"

"Man? Oh, the man who shot you? I think the police had better give you that information."

"I didn't kill him?"

"Not as far as I know. Your wife found you in the hall, called the paramedics. You lost a lot of blood, but they did a good job on you."

Kontra nodded. "This country has good medical system. Doctor?"

"Yes?"

"You can tell police I'm not well enough yet. I don't want to see them. Not yet."

"I wasn't enthusiastic about your undergoing questioning right now. I'll tell them to wait at least a day. That okay?"

"Fine. Thank you. You are good, doctor."

"I'll ask your wife to come in now."

FOUR

A candle flickered between them. Italian smells hung in the air: oregano, thyme, fennel, garlic. Jake attacked his vanilla cannoli. The dark chocolate flecks in it looked like dead ants.

"This is great. I hate the kind with candied fruit. This is vanilla cream. You only nibbled at your sandwich."

Sara wished that she smoked. It would give her something to do now that she decided to give up on the avocado, tomato, and alfalfa sprout sandwich. She hadn't been hungry after all. Surprise. She sipped her coffee.

Jake persisted. "You didn't eat."

"I'm aware of that."

"So?"

"Maybe I'm coming down with your bug."

"You look fine," Jake said.

"Thanks. Any particular reason you wanted to talk tonight?"

"I worry about you."

"I know," she said.

"You seem distant. Have anything to do with what happened yesterday?"

She regarded his cabana-boy good looks. "You've been talking with people."

"Yeah. I heard it was a freak accident, really freaky. You want to talk about it?"

She stirred her coffee for no particular reason. "No."

He chuckled.

She put the spoon down. "Oh, maybe. What's there to say?"

"How'd it happen?"

"Talk about freaking. Whip just absolutely freaked. He went buggy. Started screaming at me, and then he tried to make it up a ladder . . ."

"Ladder?"

"In that abandoned shop. The ladder broke—metal fatigue, I guess. Rust. It broke, and he fell, and for some reason this sharp metal stuff was beneath him."

"The sculpture."

"Yeah. Metal work. Welded together. The guy was impaled on a welded work of art."

"Weird."

"Not the first guy to die for art."

"It wasn't his."

Sara shrugged. "Maybe it was. I don't know. This wasn't a studio. It was a place that someone was using as a studio. Maybe it was Kool Whip's."

"Was he a sculptor?"

"Have no idea. He never let on."

"And you were chasing after him . . . why, again?"

She looked away. "God."

"Sorry."

They did not speak for at least a minute. Suddenly, Sara picked up the sandwich and took a bite, out of pure guilt.

She made a face. "Alfalfa tastes like grass."

"It *is* grass," Jake said.

"Oh." She smiled. "Yeah."

"At least I got a laugh out of you."

"Did I laugh? I didn't notice."

"You smiled. It's a start. I've seen you moody, but this . . ."

"Moodier than usual?"

Jake nodded. "What's the problem? By the way, what was Whip screaming about?"

"Besides something to the effect that he didn't clobber Smokey?"

"Besides that."

"That I was a witch. I went out and killed guys."

"Killed guys?"

"Yeah. I don't know exactly what he meant." She paused. "I guess he means the way people tend to die around me."

"Well . . ."

Sara shrugged in resignation. "It's true. I know."

"You've had some strange things happen. Things not easily explained."

"Sure have. You don't know the half of it."

"You'll have to tell me sometime," Jake said. "Sit me down and explain it all."

"Wish I could sit myself down and explain it all," Sara said.

"Anyway, I take it the accident has you down. Judging from what you say, it doesn't sound like your fault."

"It wasn't. It was just so senseless, so haphazard."

"Uh-huh."

"And it happened so fast, and there was no chance to save him, prevent it. No chance to help him after."

"Useless all the way around." Jake shook his head.

"Funny, that's what the sculptor said."

"Huh?"

"Graffiti to that effect was spray-painted on some of the best pieces. I think the artist wrote them. 'Useless junk.' And then, 'Hopeless.'"

"Maybe he was a better critic than artist?"

"Didn't look like it to me. Anyway, it was an especially senseless death. It just got to me. I'll get over it."

Jake smiled grimly. "You'll get over it. That was good."

Sara eyed him suspiciously. "You talking about the cannoli now?"

"Yeah," he said quickly. "You going to eat that sandwich?"

"You want it? I thought you had dinner. And you just had dessert."

"It looks good. I love alfalfa. I'm like a cow."

She pushed the plate toward him. "Graze away."

"Lazlo?"

He opened his eyes. Someone stood beside the bed. He got a familiar whiff of perfume. "Sophia."

"You were sleeping."

"Nothing else to do."

"They are putting you in another room tomorrow. Regular hospital room."

He gestured at the IVs and monitors. "Then I won't have these things on me?"

"Not so many. You can maybe sit up."

"Good."

She came closer. When his eyes finally focused he could see her face well enough to notice the lines. She was dressed well, as usual, bedecked with jewels. She liked diamonds, and wore them for almost any occasion. For all the make-up and miracle wrinkle cream and hair coloring, she was beginning to look a lot older, and he wondered why he had not noticed before. Or had he? He was getting old himself.

"The doctors say you are surprising them," she said. "You are getting well so soon."

"I always do."

"You are stronger than most men. But of course . . ."

"What?"

"You know," she said hesitantly.

Kontra rolled his eyes. "Oh, please."

"Baba has helped you."

He turned his head. "Again, this old nonsense."

"Do you remember the last time you were shot?"

"Yes. In Vienna."

"Baba helped you then, too."

"Baba is always helping me. She should mind her own business."

"If she did, you would be dead. This man now, he shoots you with three bullets."

"Two. Only two."

Maria looked at the ceiling. " 'Only,' he says. In your *heart*."

"They missed."

"They missed. They *didn't* miss. You had protection."

"Magic," he said with a sneer.

"You don't believe. You have never believed."

"Nonsense. Magic spells. Do you expect me to believe some old witch woman?"

"How else do you explain it?"

"Explain what?"

"That no one can kill you."

"Luck. Strength. I killed that guy."

"What guy?"

"The hit man."

"You dreamed it."

He raised his head and looked at her intently. "They didn't find him?"

"I heard you yell. I was afraid, so I listen. Then I open the door. There you were, bleeding."

"No man running?"

"I heard someone running down the stairs. Maybe. I think so."

"Did you see him?"

She shook her head.

He lay back. "Then I didn't strangle the bastard."

"How could you strangle him when he was shooting you?"

"I rushed at him and I got my hands around his neck."

She laughed. "With two bullets in you. And you doubt Baba."

He had no answer.

"Your lunch is here," she said.

"I don't want it."

"You should eat."

"I'm not hungry. Leave me, woman."

"I'll leave. Try to eat, Lazlo."

"The food is bad."

She smiled. "What hospital has good food? Tomorrow, I will bring you something from the delicatessen."

"Good. If they let you."

"I will bring it anyway."

CHAPTER
FIVE

Sara liked to walk at night in the city. She'd read something about Thomas Wolfe. Not Tom, but Thomas. He would write all day and stalk the city in the pitch of night, tramping from the Battery to the Bronx and back again.

A walk was nice, but that was a trifle extreme.

She was a little edgy tonight, and did not know why. The weather was exceptionally clear. No fog, no clouds. What few stars as could be seen from the streets of Manhattan were pinned to a velvet sky. They did their best to shine.

She stopped suddenly, and looked up, thinking she had heard something strange in the night. She searched the blackness between the buildings. Nothing moved.

She walked on. The nearest business district well behind her, she walked along a street lined with brownstones.

There it was again.

A shriek.

"What the hell is that?" she muttered. It sounded

unusually piercing, and its source seemed to be in the sky somewhere. A light plane with a loudspeaker? What?

No, it was the shriek of a bird. A screech, a caw. A cry. Like a seagull. Or maybe something else.

A plane with a loudspeaker broadcasting bird calls. Okay. Either that or a very, very large bird flying very high. A big gull?

A *really* big gull.

Whatever it was cried again. It had a particularly weird sound. There was something almost human about it. The *almost* is what made it unsettling.

She walked on, coming presently to an avenue. She stopped and looked up and down it. Was this Madison? Park? It was an unfamiliar part of one of them. Let's see, she'd started on Lexington. This should be . . . Madison. Wait. No, hadn't she passed Madison?

No traffic. Very little. Okay, it was late, but she couldn't see a headlight. Oh, wait. There's one, way the hell downtown. And a red light crawled on the horizon uptown. The cross street seemed deserted.

She looked at her watch. Okay, it must be wrong. It wasn't that late, was it? How long had she talked with Jake? She tried to remember chairs on the tables when she left. Okay, she did remember that. She thought. So tempis had fugited all over the place. But how late did that restaurant stay open? Not past eleven, surely. She wondered how long she had been walking.

Missing time?

Jeepers.

Screeeeeeeeee.

"Go away, bird."

What bird? What the hell kind of bird could be that loud and . . . and yet so high up there?

45

Scanning the sky, she continued on, and her footsteps threatened to become more hurried. So she willed herself to slow. Relax, take it easy.

Let's not completely freak out. There's absolutely nothing to be afraid of.

The Witchblade was telling her different. Its babble of voices crossed the threshold of hearing. They sometimes warned of danger. At other times they cackled with glee at the approach of something threatening. It was hard to tell whether they were for it or against it.

She stopped at the next corner, hitting a wall of confusion. She did not recognize this avenue at all. Lined with dark, faceless monoliths, it was no Manhattan thoroughfare she knew.

"What the hell?"

She stood unbelieving, casting eyes to either hand, north and south. No familiar landmark presented itself. The dark gathered between towering black shapes. They could have been buildings, but ones that offered no access to mere mortals. Their upper portions had protrusions of some kind. These were skyscrapers, but of a kind she'd never seen. Their bases were without openings, no entrances. Some towers sat on massive pylons and did not have ground floors.

Nothing made sense here. Was this some kind of housing project she had missed in the newspapers?

Something had happened to the streets themselves. They had narrowed, were now no wider than alleys.

Darkness hid any revealing detail. These presences seemed little more than geometric shapes. She was not even sure she was seeing something that existed. Only something that would exist. Or perhaps that could exist? She did not know. The images in her eyes flickered.

She closed her eyes and massaged them gently with her fingertips.

Screeeeeeeeee.

She looked up. A typical urban vista presented itself. Signs glowed reassuringly over closed shops a few streets down. Headlights crawled in the distance. The totally normal had magically reappeared. The mundane had teleported back from the alternate reality where it had been hiding.

She breathed again.

The sounds of fluttering wings made her resume her journey westward. She didn't balk at hurrying now. The Witchblade seemed disturbed, and that was enough motivation. Yes, there was a danger, but perhaps it wasn't immediate.

"Yeah," she told it. "So?"

No answer. No specifics. No guesses as to what she was facing.

At the sound of huge beating pinions she began to run. There came a rustling, a fluttering, a swooping, and the click of talons. Was she hearing it or was it in her mind? She sprinted across another wide avenue, fearful for her sanity.

The thing, whatever it was, sounded as if it had swooped close and passed directly overhead. She hadn't seen it, had felt only a strong presence, a manifestation of something strange, alien, and evil.

Evil.

Or perhaps just unknowably alien and strange. There came with this feeling a sense of intense curiosity and a need to satisfy it, to explore, to discover. To seek out and reconnoiter.

There was no fear, but there was a wariness, a caution. Nevertheless, this circumspection could not thwart

47

a resolve to fulfill a destiny. To have what was wanted, to gain it, to keep it.

The sound of its wings filled her ears as she ran. The thing swooped and swooped again, getting closer, and she could feel the wind from its wings and hear the whistle of air as taloned feet flexed and clenched, eager to grasp, to claw, to tear her apart. To rend flesh.

Evil.

She hid in shadows and felt a transformation come over her.

Wings rushed and beat like a racing heart, a darkly malevolent heart. Hovering. Hovering.

She was ready to come out into the dim light. When she did, the metamorphosis was almost complete. A filigree of delicate metal work had crawled along her body, providing her full breasts and nether portions with cover but leaving little else unexposed. Her right hand and wrist, where the bracelet had lived, and part of the forearm, were now embellished with sharp, spiky gingerbread, covering her fist in an impossible gauntlet of swirls and arabesques. She was nude and yet somehow completely covered. These geometric flourishes bloomed along other parts of her body. Up and down her long legs, around her silky thighs, covering and protecting her knees, shoulders, spine, and neck. All vulnerable points buttressed against assault. Yet wide areas of smooth skin permitted the caress of air. She was a study in dress and undress. She was a paradox.

She was the Witchblade.

Striding boldly into a pool of spilled light, she looked up and regarded the thing.

It was an enigmatic shape in the sky between the

buildings. A menacing outline, an abstract intelligence embodied in a suggestion of an avian configuration, monstrous wings flapping impossibly fast. And in the center of the phenomenon, eyes like diamonds.

She lifted the gauntlet skyward and pointed an imperious finger.

"You!" she shouted. Her voice bruised stone, made windows rattle their mullions.

The thing hovered and observed. Coolly.

She flung a question at it with resounding contempt and annoyance: *"What?"*

It continued to hover, its raptor's eyes cold and dispassionate.

Time perched somewhere else, but nearby. It waited, and watched. At some point it decided that enough eternity had occurred, and began to tick off the seconds again.

And the thing above, the indeterminate shape in the sky, began to lift, the sound of its immense wings growing into the militant beating of war drums. Its vast obscene bulk rose and receded. And with a final rustle and flutter, it disappeared into the dark sky whence it had come.

Sara stood in the middle of a deserted New York street.

She ran her hands over her leather jacket. Checked her pistol, her badge, the money in her pocket. Jingled the change. She found a piece of lint and flicked it away.

Back to good old Sara.

Old. She felt a little older after each manifestation of the Witchblade, a bit longer in the tooth. A stiffness and ache came as additional residuals, but overall it was not altogether a bad feeling. It felt a little like the afterglow of a good, vigorous gym workout, albeit one she had overdone a bit.

She walked the rest of the way home at a steady pace, not minding the shadows, unafraid, but thoughtful.

CHAPTER

SIX

It was a miracle of rare device, but it wasn't a pleasure dome. Merlin Jones's pad was more than a place to crash, having some nice stuff in it. Widescreen high-definition television, state of the art sound system. Both had fallen off trucks. Merlin had bought them at a fence's warehouse for a few hundred dollars apiece instead the thousands they cost retail. There were a few nice pieces of furniture; the couch, for one. It came from a cache of household items retained against failed payment of criminally inflated moving costs. A few other appointments around the one-room apartment were anomalously opulent. Like that massive oak bookshelf, filled to capacity.

Otherwise, the place was pretty much a mess. Stacks of books lay piled around the room, along with boxes filled to the brim with CDs, DVDs, video tapes, floppy disks, and other tech bric-a-brac. There were dozens more boxes stuffed with stolen procedure manuals from phone companies, Internet service providers, on-line brokerages, and other concerns.

Basically, the place was a dump in the Bedford-Stuyvesant section of Brooklyn.

One of the *Die Hard* movies was playing on the HDTV, running through the DVD deck. Merlin wasn't watching. He was doing what he usually did, typing on his keyboard.

The sound system crashed and banged with alternative rock of some esoteric kind. Someone was screaming obscenities.

He found it distracting. He picked up a remote and clicked it until the system breathed a sigh of relief and settled down to Mozart on the piano.

"K. 525," Merlin said to himself, still typing. It was a piano and orchestra piece.

The apartment door burst open and two big guys walked in. Merlin looked up. He knew them: Anton and Sergei. Two Russians, both wearing expensive leather jackets, shiny brown and shiny black.

"Jones," one of them said.

"Yeah," Merlin said.

"You come back to work?"

Merlin put his eyes back on the screen. "No."

"That's not good."

"Sorry." Merlin wasn't very sorry.

"You have to come back to work. Mr. Kontra is angry with you."

"I'm pretty angry with Mr. Kontra."

"He got shot, you know."

"I didn't shoot him," Merlin said.

"We know," the big Russian said. "But you refuse to work. We need you."

"Uh-huh," Merlin said, unconcerned.

"We pay you lots of money."

"Not enough. I'm putting in sixty, seventy hours a week. I either need time for my own projects or more pay for the work I do. I told him that."

The other one, the blond one with the black jacket, spoke. "You better come back to work."

"Can't. Have my own projects. Interesting stuff. It won't pay immediately, but I need to work on them."

"What can we say? What can we do?" The brown jacket sauntered over.

"Not a lot, Boris."

"How come you call me 'Boris' all the time? My name is Anton."

"Not a lot, Anton."

"Too bad," Anton said. "He needs you to work. Credit cards."

"I must have given him ten thousand good numbers. Corporate accounts. If you keep charges below a hundred bucks apiece, they'll never even know the numbers have been stolen. They might never find out. They're all big companies."

Anton shrugged. "Too many transactions. Too much bother."

Merlin sighed. "You guys." He shook his head.

"We need more numbers. More accounts."

"Yeah, well . . ."

Anton turned to his partner. "Okay, Sergei."

Sergei tipped the bookcase and half the books slid off and hit the floor.

Merlin regarded the mess casually. "What do you think you're doing?"

"He's clumsy," Anton said. "Don't do that, Sergei. Let that go."

53

Sergei let the bookcase crash to the floor.

"The downstairs neighbors are always complaining," Merlin said.

He kept typing.

"You don't want to piss off Mr. Kontra."

"I thought he was already pissed off," Merlin said.

"He is," Anton told him. "Hey, you like *Star Wars*." He was standing in front of a poster.

"Yeah. May the Force be with you, and kick the shit out of you."

Anton laughed. "Hey, *we* kick the shit out of *you*."

"I have other friends," Merlin said.

"Yeah?"

"Yeah. Militant friends. They wouldn't take it kindly if you mess with me personally. They don't like it when white guys mess with black guys. Want me to call them?"

"We don't mess with you personally. Hey, Sergei, are we going to bother him personally?"

"Not personally," Sergei said before he threw the Boze against the wall with a lot of force.

"Hey!" Merlin said. "That was one expensive piece of equipment."

"We know." Now Anton was looking at a table filled with candles. "What's this?"

"I'm pagan."

"What's that?"

"An ancient Celtic religion."

"Oh, you worship devil, uh?"

He and Sergei laughed.

"Get stuffed, guys."

Sergei picked up the DVD player.

Merlin scowled. "Put that down, you fool."

Anton asked, "You coming back to work?"

"No."

The DVD didn't break the HDTV screen, but the impact made the screen go dark.

"Shit," Merlin said, jumping up. "Hey . . ."

"That's what it is," Anton said. "Now it's big piece of shit, that TV. You need to get it fixed."

Merlin crossed the room and picked up the DVD player. He shook it. It rattled. He looked for the TV remote, found it, and thumbed a button. The TV switched over to cable and showed CNN. He breathed.

"Next time we bust it," Anton said.

Merlin sighed. "Okay."

"Okay? You come back to work?"

"I'll metaphorically come back to work."

"Eh?" Sergei looked confused—not exactly out of the norm for him.

"I'll log on."

Anton smiled. "That's good. Let's go, Sergei."

The two Russians left, neglecting to close the door.

Merlin threw the busted DVD into a corner and closed the door. He went back to his computer desk. They wouldn't touch the computer. They knew that would put him out of touch and out of business.

He sat, dumped out of what he was doing, and called up another file. Fingering the mouse, he caused the file to print. His ink jet printer whined and rolled out a sheet.

He picked it up. The white paper bore a brightly colored mandala of unusual complexity and design. He studied it.

"Magic," Merlin Jones said with a big grin.

They had put him in a private room. It was nice, and probably cost a mint per day. He could afford it. He wasn't worried. His man Anton had put some men on to guard the room. Good thing the waiting room was right across the hall. They could sit there and watch.

Anton appeared in the doorway.

"I was just thinking of you," Kontra said.

Anton walked in, hands in his pockets. "How are you today?"

"Pretty good. I must look like hell. I don't know when they will let me shave."

"You don't look so bad. You maybe should grow a beard."

"I'd look like Rasputin."

Anton chuckled. "We talked to Merlin."

"Oh? Did he see reason?"

"Yes."

"Good."

"He is a weird one."

"Ah," Kontra said, leaning his head back. He inhaled sharply, still feeling the aftereffects of the attack. "God damn this."

"It's rough," Anton said.

"Yeah. Rough."

"I wanted to tell you, the cops are here."

"Again?"

"I told the woman you didn't want—"

"Woman?"

"Woman cop from homicide."

"Homicide."

"Yeah, they sent her. I told her you were still feeling like hell."

"She went away?"

"No, she's talking to the doctor, but she's insisting on seeing you."

"Let her come in. I don't know why they bother."

"They probably know it was Italians."

"Shut up," Kontra snapped.

"Sorry."

"Maybe you want to tell them they want a piece of the moving business. Anything to do with trucks, they want their cut. You ought to tell her our whole business. Where is she?"

Looking sheepish, Anton peeked out the door. "Still talking."

"All right, send her in."

"I'll go tell her."

"Besides," Kontra said to himself, "it wasn't Italians."

The woman was surprisingly good-looking. Tall, thin, flowing hair, outstanding face. Big bosom. Dressed like beggar, though. He didn't like that. But he liked her.

"Mr. Kontra." Nice voice, too.

"Come in."

"I'm Detective Sara Pezzini, NYPD Homicide Division."

"Why Homicide? Do I look dead?"

"Well, you see . . ."

"Wait until I shave. I look a lot better." He immediately felt himself warming up to her. She looked magnificent. He took an instant shine.

"What kind of name is Kontra? Russian?"

"My mother was Russian. My father Romanian."

"So you're Romanian."

"I am an American."

The woman acknowledged the point with a smile. "Do you know who shot you, Mr. Kontra?"

"Somebody shot me?" He was all innocence.

She winced. "Wow, you are really going to make me work, aren't you?"

"Sorry. What was question again?"

"You took two .32 caliber slugs in the chest. Do you know who put them there?"

"A man."

"A man. Could you describe him?"

Kontra shrugged. "Medium height, about . . . oh, maybe thirty."

"Hair?"

"He had hair." Kontra's mouth twisted wryly. "Dark."

"Dark, like black, or brown?"

"There was no light in the hall."

"Really? I went up there. Lots of light, even at night."

"Okay, so there was light. I didn't get good look at him."

"What was he wearing?"

"A coat. Light."

"Okay, medium, about thirty, dark brown hair. Wearing a light coat. That's not a lot of help, Mr. Kontra. Could you describe his face?"

"No."

"You can't, or won't?"

"Can't. No memory. Bad memory."

"You're making it hard for us, Mr. Kontra."

"Can't help."

"What do you do for a living?"

"Businessman."

"What business?"

"Moving van and real estate."

"I see. Mr. Kontra, we think it was a mob hit."

He did his best to look shocked. "What?"

"Mob hit. An assassination attempt. You were lucky. They'll probably try again."

Kontra flipped over a hand. "This is new to me."

"Okay," the detective said with finality. "We just wanted to check it out. I suppose it's useless to ask if you recognized him."

"Never saw him."

"He was probably from out of town, anyway."

No, he wasn't, Kontra thought. He didn't rate that.

She took a stroll around the room. "We pretty much know your run-ins with the established crime families. The Sicilian crime families. You've had dealings with them in the past. And you've come into conflict."

"You know so much," Kontra said.

"Thanks. I don't know a lot of the specifics. It's not my line of work, organized crime. But I do know that you are a prominent member of what's called the *Organizatsiya*. The Russian version of the Cosa Nostra, call it what you will. You're a crime boss. Not a big time one, but one who's been up-and-coming for a long time. I read a file on you."

"They have a file on me?"

"A pretty big one. They think you've branched out into computer crime."

"I don't own a computer."

"But you are a crime boss. You still have ties to Eastern Europe."

"I have lots of relatives back there."

"And business associates. In Poland, Bulgaria, Hungary, Romania, Germany, and, of course, Russia."

"You really read this file?"

"I got a pretty good briefing this morning from the Organized Crime Task Force. These are nice flowers, by the way."

"Are you married?" he asked. This woman intrigued him.

"No. Are you?"

"Yes. Her name is Sophia. Tell me something."

She spun around. "Yes?"

"Why do you dress like a boy?"

She looked down. "This is boy stuff?"

"Or a bum's. You should wear a dress."

She raised an eyebrow. "And spike heels? I have to move when I work."

"Women today." He shook his head.

"Let's stick to the subject."

"You have a boyfriend?"

"Mr. Kontra, I know you're curious as to why I'm here, and I'm going to tell you."

Kontra shrugged amiably. "Okay."

"We were interested in a description of the hit man to see if it matched the few we have on file. We want to know if he was local or imported. And you've pretty much led us up a blind alley. I'm here simply because Homicide has to ask questions in a case like this."

"You have duty," Kontra said.

"Precisely."

"I can't blame you. Will you have dinner with me some night?"

She looked at him curiously.

He returned the stare; presently, he said, "Eh?"

"I was just trying to remember if I've ever been hit on from a hospital bed. I don't think so. I was never a nurse or hospital aid. No, I think this is a first."

"Do you like Rachmaninoff?"

"Why?"

"There is concert coming up, New York Philharmonic. There is new young soloist playing. I like him. I saw his first performance in St. Petersburg when I went back after Soviet Union fall. I want to go. You go with me?"

"Should I sit next to your wife or on your other side?"

He grinned slyly. "Whichever you wish."

"No thanks, Mr. Kontra. Nice of you to ask."

"He is playing the Second Concerto. My favorite."

"I actually prefer the Third."

"Oh, you know Rachmaninoff?"

"I have a few CDs."

"Then you should go."

She paused, seemed to consider the offer. "I might. When is it?"

"Oh, next Thursday night. I think"

"Ten to one the Philharmonic has a web page. I'll look it up."

"You like classical, then?"

"A little. Actually, my true love is alternative rock."

Kontra made a face.

"I used to be an advance person for a rock band. Before I went to the police academy. We toured Europe. It was fun. Anyway, I'll check the symphony web page."

"You do that." Kontra was amazed she showed any interest at all. He had naturally expected a cold refusal. This little sop she had thrown him was a surprisingly positive sign.

"You Russian guys are normally quiet about your business," she was saying. "But recently, there's been some bloodletting. Do you know how many unsolved gang-style homicides we have in our files?"

"Lots, I guess."

"Lots. And lots of cases have Russian names."

"Then you should go to the concert with me."

"Maybe I will. But you've been shot. Do you really think you'll be well enough in a week?"

"In a week I'll be doing gymnastics."

"You must be strong."

"You won't be able to tell me from Nadia Comaneci."

She grinned at him. "Let's hope I can."

SEVEN

Kontra woke up with a start, half expecting to see the policewoman again. My God, what had he done, asking her out? Was he crazy?

Yes, probably.

He kept falling asleep, jumping awake. He didn't have a clear idea of how long he'd been in this place. A week? Only three days? Time had become meaningless.

Crazy, asking her to go out with him. He must be mad. But she was powerfully beautiful.

Something loomed off to his left, just out of sight. A tall shape in the corner of his eye.

He jumped.

It was his grandmother.

"Baba," he said.

"How are you feeling?" Baba asked. "You look bad."

"I got shot, you crazy old woman."

"They tried to kill you."

"I think we can assume. Why are you hovering around like that, like some ghost in an old house? Come over here in front of me, please."

The old woman moved into view. She was tall and gaunt and had hair the color of fright—stark white, with hints of waxy yellow. Yet her face was still handsome, in a spooky, wrinkled way. She dressed in traditional garb, or as close to it as twenty-first century America would allow. Whatever she wore, it was drab, colorless, and had a tattered look, even when it wasn't tattered. And that babushka. Kontra hated babushkas. Always had. It made women look old before their time.

"They tried to kill you," she said.

"I think we've established that. Who do you think it was?"

"Should I know your business?"

"Do you think it was the Italians?"

"No."

He looked into her piercing blue eyes. She had no education, but she had a mind like a lighthouse. Like a beam that swept around and illuminated things far away. She was like that. "No? They don't want me out of the way?"

"They are not what they used to be. They would like to make trouble for you, but they have other problems. It was someone you know."

"That I figured. You mean in my crowd?"

"It was a rival."

"Ah. That is not a revelation from scripture. Who? That is the question."

"I will find out. I will tell you."

"Good. Bury a potato in the backyard at the full moon. Dance naked."

She glowered. "All the time you laugh at me."

"Your spells work. I'm not laughing. They shot me. For

64

the second time, the bullets didn't find my heart. Or anything. They cut them out, and I'm fine."

"Of course. You will be protected. You laugh at me, but I'm sworn to protect you. Your mother made me promise before she died, before the German bombs fell."

"Yes, yes." He had heard the story too many times. Suddenly his eyes shut. This sleepiness was getting out of hand.

"That woman."

He opened his eyes again. "What?"

"That woman," Baba said. "She is beautiful, do you think?"

"What woman? Oh. Yes."

"I know of her. She is a devil."

"What? Are you insane?"

"She is a demon-lover. She sleeps with incubus."

"Stop talking nonsense."

"Did you see the bracelet?"

"What bracelet?"

"The one she wore. It is so powerful it made my teeth hurt. She is demon herself."

"She is a policewoman."

"Perhaps. I knew of her before I saw her. She is a tool of the spirits. They use her."

"I thought she was a powerful demon," he said pointedly.

"She is, but she is also a tool of more powerful spirits. From hell."

"Oh, I see."

"You laugh again."

"I'm not laughing. Do you see me laughing?" Kontra shook his head. "Such an insane old bat."

"You were always disrespectful. You will believe anything but me. You believed the communists since you were a child."

"I was young. I think I stopped believing when I was about sixteen. After that, it was just a job."

"You believe anything but the old wisdom. What the gypsies know."

"You're not a gypsy."

"I am an old woman. I learned."

"What about this police girl? She is in league with the devil?"

"I must find out more about her."

"Find out. Please, Grandmother."

"You're going to do *what*?"

Joe Siry almost swallowed his cigarette butt. He spat it out, picked it up off the desk. It was out, so he threw it into the wastebasket.

"How many packs a day do you smoke, Joe?" Sara asked.

"Don't start with the smoking thing," he said. "What did you say you and Lazlo Kontra were going to do together?"

"He asked me to a concert."

"What, a rock concert?"

"No, classical. New York Philharmonic."

"And you're going with him?"

"Tickets are hard to come by. I haven't gone to a symphony concert in years. I figured it was about time."

"What, you've taken a fancy to gangsters?"

Sara smiled tightly. "We know next to nothing about the newest gangs. The ethnic ones. The Russian is the newest. Well, maybe not the newest. Maybe there are ones we don't even know about yet."

"What's to know about them? They all live in Brooklyn. They've been pouring into the country since the Soviet Union closed up shop."

"That I know. I was thinking about getting some deep background. We have at least six suspected contract killings unsolved that might be Russian-related."

"And you figure he's going to tell you something, what, over cocktails before, or maybe late supper after? He's going to turn state's? Gonna pull a Gravano?"

"We don't have any leads in any of those killings, Joe. Maybe I can tease one out."

He regarded her sardonically. "Interesting word you used."

She shot him an annoyed look. "You know what I mean. This is a unique opportunity. He came way out of left field. I've never . . . I mean, he just sprung it on me, and it took me a few seconds to see it as an opportunity. A Mafia don dating a cop. It's like *The Sopranos*."

Siry scowled at her. "I never saw anything about . . . oh, you mean like it's being a security risk for him?"

"This isn't a thing you'd write in a TV script. No one'd believe it. But this guy is a wild card. If he's willing to get social with a cop, we should take advantage."

"Yeah." Siry appeared to be digesting it. "Maybe. But he's not a don. First of all, he isn't even Russian. He's Bulgarian."

"Romanian."

"Whatever. And he's ex-KGB. He's not like most of the Russian gangsters. Most of them are thugs with lots of prison time. This guy has education, and he was smart

67

enough to bail when he got into trouble, way back in the Eighties. He's clean. He's a born criminal mastermind. He can't be dumb enough to spill something on a social occasion."

"I'm not so sure."

"Not so sure about what?"

"That I can't find out something useful. Few cops ever socialize . . ." Sara's voice trailed off. "Hmmm. I better not say anything."

Siry laughed. "Yeah, you better not. Seltzer might have a bug in here."

"I wouldn't put it past him. Anyway, I view it as a unique undercover opportunity, in a way."

"You make it sound as if he's going to show you his books. If he keeps any."

"I'm telling you, Joe, I want to do it."

"Okay. I don't know what I'm going to tell Seltzer."

"Why does he have to know?"

"You know he oversees undercover operations. Makes sure our guys don't get carried away with their role-playing."

"This isn't undercover. I'm not playing any role. I'm going on a date with the guy."

"Wait a minute. Where did I put that file . . . ?" Siry rummaged through the scrum of paperwork on the desk-top, came up with a sheet. He eyed it a moment, then pointed at one line in particular. "Here. The guy's married. Hey, I don't know about this."

Sara glared at him. "Joe, I'm not going to *sleep* with him."

"I don't . . . jeez." Siry was nonplused.

She smiled. He was vein-popping again.

"What's so goddamn funny? Look, I can't tell you

what you can do on your own time. But there's such a thing as the appearance of . . . of . . ."

"Don't worry. There's not going to be an appearance of anything. He's not my type."

"I don't give a damn about whether he's your type. I'm worried about what it's going to look like."

"Yeah, so many cops have season tickets to the symphony."

"You are a wiseass, you know that?"

"Yes, sir."

The office door creaked open and Jake McCarthy stuck his head in. "Joe, did you want to see—Oh, hi, Pez."

Siry jerked his thumb at Sara. "Know she has a date with a Mafioso?"

Jake stepped in, his jaw hanging. "Huh? Sara, is that right?"

Sara ignored him. "The Task Force summary talked about another term—Russian, what was it? 'Chief Thief' is the translation. No, that isn't it. I have the brief on my desk."

Jake said, "What did you say, Joe?"

"She's going out with a gangster."

"Huh?"

"She's going undercover."

"Watch how you phrase that," Sara warned.

"Huh?"

Siry threw his arms up at McCarthy. "Are you going to keep saying 'huh'?"

"Huh? I mean . . ."

Sara rose. "I gotta go. The concert isn't for a couple of days, so there's no hurry about this."

"Pez, uh . . . how about a cup of coffee?"

" 'Thief-in-law,' " she said, snapping fingers.

"Huh?" Joe Siry said.

Jake looked at him.

"That's the translation of the Russian term for crime boss," Sara explained. " 'Thief-in-law.' I forget what the Russian phrase is. But Kontra didn't start out that way. The way I figure it, organized crime could only exist with high-level Soviet corruption. Kontra was probably a cop on the payroll, then became a player himself. But now he's *capo* of his own little family."

"Isn't that Italian?" Siry asked, frowning.

Sara shrugged. "I don't know any Russian."

"I'm really sorry I sent you for the interview," Siry told her. "I gave it to you because it was bound to be useless. I thought you couldn't get into trouble. But . . ."

Sara said, "But?"

"Since you're taking such an interest, I might as well loan you out to the Task Force temporarily. I put in a request for better coordination with the division. I don't know, though . . ."

"Are you still bothered by that accident?"

"Forget it," Siry said. "I backed you up."

"I know you did," Sara said. "I appreciate it. But there's still going to be some nosing around about it. I'm still facing a preliminary investigative interview."

"If it was an accident, it was an accident," Siry tautologized.

"It *was* an accident," Sara told him.

"Good. Remember that the Task Force is hooked up to the DA's office. You'll be working with the same people who might indict you for involuntary manslaughter."

Sara asked, "Do you know something I don't?"

"God, I hope not. Now get out of here and leave me to my misery. McCarthy!"

"What?"

"Don't you know that when you come back from being out sick, you're supposed to report to the Watch Commander that you've returned to duty?"

"Sorry, sir. I forgot. I've been meaning to do it all day."

McCarthy gingerly closed the door after following Sara into the corridor.

"Damn," he said to himself.

"Don't beat yourself up," Sara told him.

"I hate when that happens."

"Don't worry, it doesn't happen often. You're usually a stickler for procedure."

"I've had a lot on my mind lately. And that bug sort of knocked me for a loop. Got time for a cup in the break room?"

Sara shook her head. "I want to get home. I'm bushed."

"What did you do all day? Besides hitting on Mafiosi."

He hit on *me*. No, what wore me out was writing that report on Whip. Trying to avoid making it sound ridiculous. Impossible."

"So you didn't succeed?"

"No. Nothing wears me out more than a stint in the Report Writing Room."

"Otherwise known as the Whopper Room."

"That's exactly what Seltzer is going to think."

"That you're lying? That you threw Whip off that balcony? Whip wasn't a big dude ... I mean, everybody knows you can handle yourself as well as any guy, Sara, but ... well, you know, you ... uh ..."

Jake looked thoughtful. Obviously, something at the back of his mind had been nattering at him as he spoke.

She looked at him clinically. "See? You have your doubts about me, too."

"Hey, wait a minute," Jake was in a hurry to say. He tried to touch her arm as she suddenly turned and stepped away. She was too quick.

"Never mind," she snapped.

"Wait, wait . . . I didn't mean . . ."

"Forget it," Sara said over her shoulder.

CHAPTER
EIGHT

After spending the early evening at the public library doing some light research (she found a good book on the new ethnic gangs), Sara ate alone at a fast burger place, perversely ordering salad and a baked potato. Then she went home and watched TV for three solid hours, not realizing how much time was passing.

Finally, she clicked the TV off and got up, looked at the clock. "What a waste."

She sat at her computer, logged onto her ISP, and got her e-mail. She had three news service downloads and six commercial spam messages. No real messages. She deleted everything and logged off.

She sat and stared at the notebook computer's dead screen.

Cops don't have many friends, she realized as she brushed her teeth. Outside the force, that is. You try to mix in, you try to socialize with civilians, but as soon as you let loose what you do for a living, it kind of hangs there in the middle of the conversation like a huge icicle,

and the temperature suddenly drops ten degrees. Someone makes a feeble joke. And over the next five minutes,
you find that everyone has an excuse to move to the
other side of the room. And you find yourself sitting
alone with a stale drink, smiling stiffly.

And for her, it was usually worse. Men's pupils became
pinpoints; they coughed and look away. Cop? Did she say
cop? And a detective, yet.

The only thing worse, she'd been told, is for a woman
to say she is a deputy district attorney; or worse yet, a
judge.

Do all civilians have guilty consciences? Seemed so, at
times.

It didn't bother her much. She rarely thought about
such things. Only on occasion. By the time she finally
crawled into bed, it was out of her mind entirely.

She woke. A weird glow filled the room, a faint spectral
light, growing brighter, suffused with a pale greenish tint.
Her eyes, adapted to dark, saw it as painfully bright.

Naked, she rose from the bed. The light emanated from
her desk. It quickly became apparent that she had left the
notebook on, though she could swear that she'd turned it
off well before going to bed.

Odd geometrical bands of light played across the
screen. The display looked like an elaborate screen saver,
forming bright patterns and figures that constantly
moved and shifted: concentric circles and squares, moires
and zigzags, waves and grids, reticulated fields, all radi-
ating a pale blue-green aura that tinted the walls.

She approached it carefully. When had she loaded this
program? It must be something that downloaded itself
from the Internet, unbeknownst to her.

A virus!

No computer of hers had ever caught a virus before. She was fascinated, in a way. She wanted to find out more about such rarefied phenomena. She wondered what she should do. Turn the machine off? Probably. Bring it to the precinct, let some expert in the white collar crime section take a look at it? Maybe it was a new virus no one had ever seen before.

The patterns on the screen grew busier, more complex. They interlaced and interweaved; they danced and cavorted, then, inexplicably, burst out of the screen and spilled across the desk, the floor, the walls.

She jumped back.

She froze as the pale green lines flowed around her and took her measure, calibrating and quantifying her every dimension. She felt nothing, but there was something strangely palpable about this light. It had a substance of some kind, she was sure. She felt a presence in it. And all at once she somehow knew this manifestation for what it was: lucent nerves in a sensorium cast out like a web by an unimaginable being far removed. She did not know what kind of being. She was not sure she wished to find out.

A cage of light surrounded her, shifting and flowing over her skin, gauging her, evaluating her. It lingered for several seconds, then moved toward her bed, there to coalesce around something on the nightstand.

The Witchblade.

She watched as the lines of light played across the bracelet. It seemed to resist. The stone glowed brightly, its light throwing a warm backdrop for the cold, alien display. The room came alive with weird color.

She made a move toward the nightstand. Something

held her back. An adjunct structure of some sort extended from the green cage surrounding the bracelet and became force as well as light. Ghostly arms of restraint blocked her, held her back.

She struggled but couldn't make any progress. The glow from the bracelet intensified.

She let out a groan and fell to the bare wood floor, strapped by unseen fetters. The lines of light felt like electricity now, crackling across her bare skin. Prickly threads of static pinned her under a net of force.

She managed to crawl a few inches. She could make progress a little at a time. Painfully, she got to her knees. The floor felt like a griddle, frying her kneecaps. She pushed forward toward the nightstand, reaching a hand upward.

There commenced loud crackling and discharge. Blinding flashes and displays leapt up all around her. It was as if a hundred loose high-tension power lines were whipping around the room, arcing and throwing sparks.

A whirlwind of fire surged from the Witchblade, engaged the pale green grid in a struggle of tension, and a contest between bright displays of color and energy began. Sara kept reaching, trying to touch the bracelet. She could not quite make it.

The battle continued for a full minute. Then, abruptly, the green forces seemed to lose vitality and began an orderly withdrawal to the screen, fighting a rearguard action. Pale fingers of luminescence dimmed and retreated, backing along walls, ceiling, and floor.

Sara finally made contact with the bracelet, grabbed it, and put it on her right wrist. She sat up and looked at the computer.

The green lines were back on the screen. Gradually, they faded; but the screen continued to glow eerily.

She saw faces in it. She thought she saw faces. Strange, inhuman faces.

No, not inhuman. She looked again. They were . . . non-human. Humanoid. Humanish. No, human-like. Simulacra, artifacts, constructs. They weren't really alive. Those . . . things, there, could not have life in the normal sense. They were parodies of that which was human.

The eyes. She could not bear to look into their eyes.

Did she see them or was she imagining? She passed a palm across her face and looked again.

The screen was faintly glowing now. Fading.

Screeeeeeeee.

She did not know where the hell-bird's cry had come from, the sky or the screen. She looked out a window but saw nothing but blankness over the city.

By the time she had put on a robe and walked to the desk, the screen was completely dark, and the computer was not operating. She suppressed a motion to turn it on. Perhaps she should let it rest. She carefully lowered the screen and clicked it shut.

She didn't bother looking at the clock. She knew it would be a long, long wait until morning, and that she would be up the whole time.

"Mr. Kontra, this is amazing."

"What?"

The doctor leafed through a sheaf of reports. Behind him stood about two dozen interns, all with baby faces. To Kontra, they looked like a kindergarten class. "Your progress is phenomenal. Only three days later, and . . ."

"I heal fast."

"I've never seen this kind of . . . these test reports."

"I feel lots better today."

The doctor turned to his charges. "I've heard of cases like this, but you people have been privileged actually to see one. Any questions?"

"How old are these kids?" Kontra wanted to know.

The doctor smiled. "They're all through medical school. We just had a conference on you. Needless to say we're very, very pleased with your progress. We should have you out of here in three days."

"I want out tomorrow." Kontra said.

"Well, that might be premature . . ."

"Tomorrow."

The doctor gave up leafing through the charts. "I'm going to order an other set of X-rays first. Then I'll let the floor nurse know. Okay?"

"Sure."

"Do you have any complaints, any symptoms?"

Kontra smiled and shook his head.

"It's like magic," the doctor said.

CHAPTER
NINE

Sara yawned, then said, "I'm sorry."

The array of gray-faced men before her seemed affronted. Gray morning light filtered through dirty windows. It was a gray world out there, and it was pretty grim in here.

"Are you having trouble sleeping, Detective?" Seltzer wanted to know.

Sara began, "As a matter of fact . . ."

"We'll try to be brief, so that you can get your beauty rest."

Flanagan, the man to Seltzer's right coughed. "I don't think we have to get into personalities," he said.

"Who's doing that?" Seltzer wanted to know.

"Let's get back to business," Flanagan said. "Ms. Pezzini . . ."

"That remark could be construed as prejudicial," Sara commented.

"What remark?"

"The one about beauty rest. Lawsuits have been brought on lesser grounds."

Flanagan fussed with his papers. "Detective Pezzini, are you threatening this board with litigation on the basis of a casual remark?"

"Blackmail's not going to get you anywhere," Seltzer told her.

"Does the term 'hostile work environment' mean anything to you?"

Seltzer scowled. "Oh my God, a locker room lawyer."

"Please, Sergeant Seltzer," Flanagan said.

"Sorry. Do go on. By the way, Detective, you might want to be diagnosed for sleep apnea. It's a condition in which—"

"Sergeant . . ." Flanagan said with a warning tone.

"Excuse me."

Flanagan cleared his throat. "Detective Pezzini."

"Yes, sir?"

"Do you have anything else by way of amplification or comment, in addition to the report you filed?"

"No, sir."

"Are you quite sure?"

"I'm quite sure."

"Anything you might have left out, however seemingly slight or inconsequential?"

"I included everything."

"I see. Well, although it looks like a pure case of death by misadventure . . ."

"That is what the coroner's inquest found," Sara reminded him.

"Uh, yes. Yes, that is indeed what the coroner's inquest—"

"Which doesn't have any bearing on the findings of this board," Seltzer said sharply. "We are here to investigate any untoward event that happens in the course of standard department procedure and to look for possible culpability on the part of any department personnel who—"

"I think," Flanagan interposed, "we all know the purpose of this board. As I was saying, although it looks as if this case can be adjudicated in your favor, Detective Pezzini, the file still has to go to the committee for final disposition. At that time you'll be informed of the committee's findings and any action that might or might not be taken. Meanwhile, this hearing is adjourned. Thank you for your cooperation."

Oddly enough, the day was brightening. Sunlight began to leak through heavy cloud cover.

Sara said, "You're welcome."

The concert hall was filled to about three-quarters capacity, for all that this concert was officially sold out. The empty seats were easy to explain: season tickets holders, high-rollers failing to show up and not deigning to let anyone else make good use of their ticket.

Sara and Kontra sat together. Two bodyguards, Anton and Sergei, sat directly behind them.

Good seats, Sara thought. Orchestra Circle, keyboard side. She would be able to see the piano soloist's hands.

The guest conductor, a diminutive Asian man whose name had beat a hasty exit from Sara's mind, walked out from the wings to enthusiastic applause. He stood at the podium and waited. There seemed to be something amiss backstage. He turned to the audience and smiled a little nervously, raising a hand as if to say, patience, please.

Presently, a tall, solidly-built man walked out and took his seat at the piano.

"Damn it," Kontra said. "This isn't new kid. Who is this?"

Sara's mouth was hanging open. Could it be?

Ian Nottingham?

It couldn't. See was seeing things again.

She listened as the pianist struck spooky, mordant chords and sounded the same deep base note after each. After the chords rose to a crescendo, piano and orchestra launched like a great, black ship into a deeply moving, quintessentially Russian melody that took the Romantic to dimensions hitherto unknown. It conjured many things: earth-curving sweeps of land, the soil, the sky, endless weeping, romance, loss and remembrance—the spirit of a vast, tragic, solemn country, distilled in a heady musical draught.

She really didn't know why, but tears instantly welled in her eyes, and she fought to keep them from spilling out.

"He was good, whoever he was," Kontra allowed afterwards, over tea and cakes. "Did you like it?"

"It was so . . . Russian," Sara said.

"Yes, Rachmaninoff. He was old Russia. A life for the Czar, big estates, complacent peasants, old money. He left after revolution and never came back. But he was true *artiste*. You said you think you know the pianist?"

"Yes. I think so. But . . ."

Kontra set his tea cup down. "But?"

"I thought he was dead."

Kontra looked at her for a moment. Then he said, "You are strange woman. Beautiful, but strange."

"Thanks," Sara said. "I think."

"I'm told you . . ." He stopped, seeming dubious about proceeding. "Well, I will say it. You are involved with some kind of magic."

Sara's distrusting frown elicited an expansive gesture of apology from him. She asked, "Where did you hear that?"

"I know a witch woman."

"What?"

"Gypsy woman. Well, she isn't gypsy. Actually, I think she has the blood. But she knows."

"Who is she, if you don't mind my asking?"

"My grandmother. *Baba* is what you call her in old country. Old woman."

"And what does she do, look into a crystal ball?"

He shrugged. "I don't know. I don't believe in such things. But she has the power to see where people can't see."

"The future? Other places?"

Kontra waved a hand vaguely. "She . . . sees things."

"Okay. And she sees me."

"Yes. She says you are witch woman, too. Are you?"

"No. I do wear this bracelet, though."

"I was noticing. I saw it when you come to hospital. I tell my grandmother. She saw it. She says it is demon thing."

"Demon thing." Sara looked at her plate. "Well . . ."

"That make it powerful. But you aren't interested in power."

"I'm not interested in power. It comes in handy, though, I will admit."

"What does bracelet do?"

"Not a lot. Oh, I meant to ask you. What happened to Anton and Sergei? When the concert ended, they weren't around." She also remembered that just before the pianist left the stage after his last bow, he seemed to look straight out at her. "When did they leave?" she asked.

"They hate classical. They like to go out to club. That's probably where they went. Meet women."

"Aren't they your . . . protection?"

Kontra shrugged. "You can't have bodyguard all the time. It's ridiculous. I'm not John Gotti. I'm not big shot. You think I am, but I'm not."

"Funny I didn't see them get up and leave. Or hear them."

"The third movement is loud."

Sara reached for her purse.

"You going?" Kontra asked.

"I have to make an early night of it."

"Really. So sad. You let me take you home?"

"No, I'll get a cab. There's someone I have to see."

"This late?"

"Thanks for the concert. I really enjoyed it."

Kontra sat back and grinned. "No more than me. Good night, Sara."

"Good night, Lazlo."

The graveyard probably dated from New York's Knickerbocker era. All old graveyards look alike: weathered headstones, faded lettering, grass grown to neglect, weeds. Foot markers covered with moss. Forlorn trees.

Her father's grave did not look bad. She had kept after it over the years, but it had been a while since her last visit. She bent to pluck a withered dandelion, threw it away. Then she stood and thought about the past.

"Hi, Dad. It's Peeps," she said to the quiet air.

Her father's pet name for her when she'd been a kid. Kontra's remark about her being a strange woman was probably true. No, it was absolutely true. When most girls tell their daddy what they want to be when they grow up, it's usually a ballerina, a princess, a nurse, a teacher—whatever. But for little Sara it was . . . a policeman. A policeman. There isn't even a good word for a policeman who isn't a man. Policewoman isn't great, and *policeperson*? Ugh.

The job never did him any good. The pay was lousy, and then you died.

She bent her head. She hadn't gotten over it yet, had she?

No. Not yet. She hadn't been there, hadn't seen it, but she had never been able to rid her mind of the image of her father lying on the street, shot by an assassin.

She had no idea how long she had stood there, contemplating her father's grave, when she heard someone call her name.

She turned. The man who had played the concerto was approaching her, his athletic figure limned in streetlight.

"Ian Nottingham," she said. "It *was* you."

"Sara. Somehow I knew you'd be here."

"You always seem to know."

He was still dressed in white tie and tails. A cape fluttered in a sudden gust of wind, along with his impressive mane of hair. She wondered how he had arranged that touch. He had always had a flair for the melodramatic.

"It's getting to be our meeting place," she said. "How have you been?"

"Fine, keeping busy. Something's up. Again."

"Again. Do you have any clues?"

"I always have clues," said Nottingham.

"You pick them up out of the air," she said. "I've always wondered if it were an innate ability, or one you acquired."

"In a way, I've always been clairvoyant. But my various

bouts of training have sharpened what paranormal skills I was born with."

"What's your reading on the current situation?"

"It is something very, very strange."

She walked to a nearby stone bench and sat down. "What do computers have to do with it?"

"Computers?" Ian Nottingham said.

"Something attacked me out of a computer."

"Whoa," Nottingham said.

"And then there's this big bird."

"Big bird," Nottingham repeated dully.

"Not the one from . . . oh, never mind. Maybe we aren't talking about the same thing."

Nottingham seated himself on the extreme opposite end of the bench. "I was only referring to a general sense of impending evil. This is what I've received. An intrusion into our world of something very alien and extremely exotic."

"Well, that sounds something like it. Whatever it is, it's very interested in the Witchblade."

"Precisely. I've sensed a struggle for control."

"Control of what?"

"Perhaps this world. Then again . . ." Nottingham looked off abstractedly.

"Go on," Sara said.

"Have you ever thought about the world in which the Witchblade originated?"

"Nothing specific about it ever comes to mind."

"But you have realized the artifact couldn't come from our world. You do realize that The Wtichblade is an entity itself, and there are no entities like it on this earth."

"One of these days," Sara said, "someone will tell me

what the Witchblade really is, definitively, once and for all, no going back. But I'm not going to hold my breath."

"Have you ever wondered if there are other entities in that world?"

"Sure."

"Furthermore, did you ever wonder if there were factions in this other world who vie for its possession?"

"You're damn right I've wondered."

"Of course. All this goes without saying. But perhaps the struggle is interworld as well as intraworld. There could be competing factions in other worlds who want the Blade."

"It's one popular little item," she said sardonically.

"Okay, that's occurred to you, too. But tunneling through from world to world is a fairly difficult proposition. It happens neither often nor easily. With me so far?"

"So far."

"Somebody's making it easy for somebody. Now, you say you were attacked out of a computer. Are you sure it was an attack, or simply a probe of some kind?"

"Could have been either or both."

"I've never heard of magic being done via a computer. But then again, there are prayer wheels."

"Prayer wheels?"

"Well, same idea. A mechanical device that facilitates a supernatural end."

"I think I see what you mean. But why do you think magic has anything to do with the current situation?"

"As far as I know, there are no technologies that can bridge the gap between the various realms of existence. Only magic can do it. Magic is merely the means of channeling energy from one realm to another."

"I think I see what you're driving at," Sara said.

"What's going on in your world now?" Nottingham wanted to know.

Sara shrugged. "Not a lot. Weird thing happened the other day . . ."

Nottingham waited.

After a moment, Sara said, "Forget it. The thing I'm doing now is nosing around a Russian Mafia gang."

"Any magical element involved?"

"Now that you mention it, yes, sort of."

"Then there's a connection."

"Yeah, if you believe an old Romanian gypsy woman."

"Romanian?"

Sara sat up stiffly. "Oh, no."

Nottingham laughed. "Romania."

"Transylvania," Sara said. "But . . . but wait a minute. All *that* stuff doesn't jibe with what's been happening. I've seen no fangs, no bats, no coffins with soil in them. Birds, Ian. Birds. Or more accurately, one huge, honking bird. How does that tally up?"

"I don't know."

"Birds, computers . . . crime. Russians." Sara let out a sigh.

"Why won't you tell me what happened the other day?"

Sara shifted on the bench. "It was an impaling. Accident, a suspect."

"Impaling?" Nottingham said with some amazement.

"Freak accident."

"Vlad."

"Huh?"

"Vlad the Impaler."

"Wait a minute," Sara said with some alarm. "Wait just a minute, now."

"He was not a vampire."

Sara's eyebrows lifted in genuine surprise. "He wasn't?"

"No. That was Bram Stoker using an historical figure to create fiction. Vlad was possibly demonic, but he didn't suck anybody's blood. However, you wanted a Romanian connection . . ."

"Wasn't he Hungarian?"

"Transylvania was then part of the Magyar empire. Vlad defended it against the Turks."

"I see. That helps, a little. Not much."

Nottingham stood. "You're on your own with this one, Sara."

Sara stood up as he walked away. "I usually am. By the way . . ."

"Yes?" Nottingham turned at the foot of the concrete path.

"Nice playing tonight."

"Evgeny took ill," he said. "I sat in."

"It was wonderful. You play marvelously."

"I'm rusty. Don't get a chance to practice."

"You're too modest."

"Thanks for the compliment. And remember something."

"Sure."

"Remember that the Witchblade is a manifestation in this world of something that we may not be able to understand in its world of origin. That goes for any appearance of the paranormal in this world. What you're seeing on this side may not be what's on the other. Good bye, Sara."

He turned and walked away into the night, cape fluttering theatrically.

CHAPTER

TEN

Merlin advanced through the beat-up neighborhood cautiously. He knew a lot of people who lived here, but that was not necessarily a good thing. Not always.

He turned a corner. All clear, so he upped his pace. The sky was blue-white, almost as bright as the sun itself. The Aslan-owned convenience stores were open, and kids played on the street. The neighborhood was the worse for wear, but wasn't a particularly bad one. Just poor.

Merlin was feeling reasonably good until a blue Mercedes pulled up sharply to the curb and two familiar Russian torpedoes spilled out.

"Yo, Merlin," Anton yelled, running.

Merlin ducked into the bar that presented itself as soon as he ran around the corner. He knew the bartender, who was bending over the sink. The rest of the place was lightly clienteled: two bar flies and three men at a table sharing a pitcher of beer. The place was dark and stank of spilled beer and splashed urine.

"My man," the bartender said to him.

"Gotta go right out the back. You mind?"

"Cops?"

"No."

"White guys?"

"Yeah."

"They ain't comin' in here."

Merlin hesitated. Might be better to stay put. The Russians didn't like to hang out in this neighborhood. They usually wouldn't follow anybody into a bar like this. But you never knew. And he didn't like to be trapped in a place.

"Thanks," Merlin said, and walked through a door in the back wall into a storage room filled with stacked beer cases. The exit door was slightly open, leaking daylight. Merlin poked his nose out. Nothing happening.

The alley was clear. Soon he got the notion that Anton and Sergei thought he was still in the bar and were probably watching the front. They weren't altogether the brightest guys on the face of the planet.

His cell phone burbled and he took it out of his pocket. He had e-mail, but judging from the address of the sender, he didn't bother to open it now. It was just chat.

There she was again. A woman he'd been seeing around the neighborhood. She filled out her jeans very well, and Merlin extrapolated the curve in his mind. She walked past the end of the alley, and he exited and followed.

His phone beeped again. He ignored it. She heard it, and turned, gave him a smile. He liked her face. *Now, who are you, girl?*

The phone wouldn't quit, so he took it out and flipped it open. " 'Lo?"

"Merlin."

"Yeah?" The voice was unpleasantly familiar.

"Turn around."

Before he did, he knew it was Anton, driving the

Mercedes, creeping along close to the curb. Anton waved and smiled.

Merlin ran past the tight-jeaned woman and got about a quarter-block before Sergei stepped out from the next alley and grabbed him.

The door of the apartment flew open and Merlin lurched in. Blood covered the front of his suede jacket and his face was puffed up and discolored. His left eye had swollen shut. Blood ran from his mouth.

He stumbled into the bathroom and splashed water on his face. He stared at himself in the mirror. Then he ripped off his ruined clothes and stepped into the shower.

He let hot water steam him for twenty minutes. He stepped out and covered himself with a white terrycloth robe. He took a look in the mirror. The swelling had gone down. He looked and felt one hundred percent better, but his face and ribs still hurt.

He sat at his computer and typed. He liked to sit at his computer and type. He'd been doing it since his early teens, which was not all that far in the past. He hit the keys savagely. Colors began to dance on the screen.

The bully boys had always had it in for him. Always. They were all alike, white or black. He would have felt guilty about letting white guys beat him up if so many black ones hadn't done the same thing. He could never defend himself very well, but that didn't mean he was . . . well, what they always called him. He *liked* women. The bastards. The bastards.

He kept jabbing keys.

Sara finally found the place, a small oil distribution company in south Brooklyn. It looked more like a junkyard with some of the junk cleared away. There wasn't much to the non-junk part: a few large elevated tanks covered with rust spots, one or two sheds, a trailer, and three delivery tankers parked in a small lot. The outfit sold home heating oil. If the Organized Crime Task Force report was correct, it bought product in states with low fuel taxes and sold it in New York, which had whopping fuel taxes. The margin of saving was pure profit. Which was purely illegal of course. A common enough dodge, but an extremely lucrative one.

Sara parked the division car and walked through the gate, showing her badge to the uniformed officers who had set up a crime scene perimeter.

As she walked toward the trailer, where a clot of crime scene techs and a few plainclothes had gathered, she saw someone from the Task Force she recognized, Dave Lambert.

"Sara."

"Dave. Got your report. Thanks."

"Sorry to take another case off your hands, but we're mighty interested in this one. So's the FBI."

"Are they here?"

"No, they trust us on some things."

Sara looked at all the techs roving around the yard. "Looks like you're doing a thorough job. Believe me, I have a big enough workload. I have to make a report, though. Who's the victim?"

"Guy by the name of Ashkenazi. He was running a pretty big fuel tax evasion operation here. Somebody whacked him."

"Know who?" Sara said casually.

"Yeah. I think so. I think it was payback for an attempted hit last week. The one on Lazlo Kontra."

"You have a time of death yet?"

"Tennish, last night. Uh, you look thoughtful."

"Hm? Oh, nothing. Go ahead."

"Well, looks like he was here alone, working late. He was a hands-on kind of guy. Didn't like bodyguards much. He was a tough old nut, veteran of Soviet prisons."

"What did he have against Kontra?"

"Near as I can find out, it goes back to the old country. They were enemies of long standing. What I got from informants was that Kontra strangled Ashkenazi's brother, long time ago."

"Strangled?"

"Yeah. Never did find out the details. It was pure vendetta, this one. Well, they're all vendettas in a way. Way of life with these people."

"Know who did the whack?"

"Well, if it wasn't one of Kontra's soldiers, I don't know who it was. Small-caliber pistol left at the scene. Serial number will probably lead nowhere."

"You seem pretty sure about all the facts. Think you can pick up anybody?"

"Possible we might get some forensic links. Let's say have enough to get a warrant to haul in both his top henchmen. Before you know it, they'll produce witnesses who'll perjure themselves to provide an ironclad alibi. You find a whole bar full of people in Brighton Beach who'll submit affidavits. Say they bought the suspects drinks all night and that they never left the table."

And of course their boss will have a different alibi, Sara thought.

"We've been down this road before," she said. "You'd think Kontra wouldn't use two of his closest associates."

"Sara, this isn't the big time. No fifty-thousand-dollar

contract killers flown in. Everything's pretty much done in-house with this crowd."

She didn't spend long inside the trailer. Ashkenazi did not look to have suffered before he died. Nevertheless, she couldn't help interpreting the expression on the corpse's face as relief that it was all over. No more struggling, no more jail time, no more time, for all time.

And now to look up Kontra and have a chat.

She had a bone to pick with him.

ELEVEN

H ave another?" asked the bartender.

"Sure," Sara said.

"Same?"

"Gee and tee with lime. No piano player tonight?"

"Coming up. No, he's off Tuesdays."

The place was packed, anyway. Maybe he wasn't such a good piano player. Or played stuff nobody wanted to hear. She tried to imagine Nottingham playing a Billy Joel tune, or maybe doing an Elton John riff. She couldn't. But she really did not know enough about the man's musical tastes to hazard a guess. She did know that he was the only other person of her acquaintance who could wear the Witchblade and live.

"Haven't seen you around before," the bartender overtured.

She'd been wondering when he would get around to it. He seemed a little wary of her. Why, she didn't know, but as this was a bar which Russian wiseguys were known to frequent, he might have figured she belonged to one.

She tried to imagine herself a gangster's moll. She could not.

Actually, she had always been more inclined to imagine herself a gangster. Ma Barker, maybe. Bonnie, of Clyde fame. That was more like it, if she were to indulge in that sort of thing. But cop fantasies had always taken precedence. She could no more fancy herself a minion of the forces of evil than a mongoose could daydream about being a cobra.

"Never get to Brooklyn much," she told the bartender.

"Oh? What's the occasion tonight?" A little on the young side of thirty, he was smiling. He wasn't bad-looking.

"Looking for a friend."

"Yeah? Who? I might know him."

"Actually two guys. Two Russian guys, with accents."

The bartender laughed. "Around here . . ."

"Yeah," she said. "I know. One of them is named Sergei."

The smile vanished. The guy shrugged. "Yell that name here, six guys are going to answer."

"And the other is Anton."

"Oh, yeah." The bartender frowned almost imperceptibly. "I know them. They haven't been in tonight. Not yet, anyway."

"They usually stop in?"

"Late, usually. They friends of yours?"

"Not exactly. Acquaintances."

"Uh-huh."

He was mentally backing off now, sensing something he didn't trust or like.

"Look," she said. "No way you're not going to tip them off now, so I'll tell you that I'm NYPD Homicide."

"Yeah?"

"I've tried to contact their boss, but he's disappeared. Now I'm looking for them. If you see them, tell them I'm going to pick them up eventually. Meanwhile, I want their address."

The bartender threw his arms wide. "From me?"

"Just tell me where they live."

"I don't know them from Adam. Not really. They just come in every once in a while."

"Not what I heard. I heard they practically live here."

"Oh?"

"In here every night, without fail. Now, where the hell are they? I'm tired of waiting."

"They didn't come in."

Sara leaned across the bar. "We've established that, dude. Now, where do they live? They must have mentioned it sometime."

He didn't dare cast eyes on her cleavage, but was having a hard time resisting. "Look, I don't want any trouble."

"Then just tell me where Anton and Sergei live."

"Upstairs."

"How convenient. Is there a back way?"

"Yeah. Just go past the rest rooms. Take these keys. I sometimes go up there and take care of things for them."

"You always so kind to people you don't know from Adam?"

She got up from her bar seat.

"Hey, don't you need a search warrant?"

"You offered me the keys."

"Uh, I didn't . . . I didn't mean—"

"Thanks."

The bracelet had been throbbing faintly all evening. As she climbed the stairs it began to thump like a bass drum.

The stairs showed use. No footprints in dust. They were clean and free of junk and must have been used by the thugs regularly, if not by their houseboy downstairs.

She tried the first key on the ring she'd been given. It didn't fit. The second didn't either, but the smallest one threw aside a deadbolt inside the jamb. It was louder than she wanted it. She waited for some reaction inside.

Silence.

She pushed the door open and stared into a dark apartment. Spilling streetlight outlined a small living room.

"Anyone home?" she called out.

The darkness did not answer. She took a step in and called again and got the same response. She closed the door and felt the wall for a switch. She didn't find one, and had to inch her way across the carpeted floor. As she did, she wished for her jacket and jeans and their many pockets instead of this cocktail dress and silly pocketbook that could barely hold her keychain, which, by the way, had a tiny penlight . . .

She crunched something underfoot.

The Witchblade came alive and began to babble.

She moved forward and kicked something, sending it skittering across the floor. She could now see some kind of upset in the room. The place was a shambles, and as her eyes adapted to the dark, she could see the vast extent of it. The furniture was all overturned, debris littered the floor. She walked on broken glass and scattered paper.

Fumbling in her pocketbook, she wondered where the damned light switches were. There, across the room, by that alcove that went into another area or room. Finally reaching the other side, she still failed to find a switch but got the penlight to work. It cast a feeble beam over the room.

She gasped.

The place looked like a tornado had gone through it. The beam revealed things she was sure she didn't want to see in detail. Things that looked like blood, pools of blood. Through a daze of a shock that reached through her tough hide for such things, she saw heaps of entrails . . .

The Witchblade yammered at her.

Her foot slipped in something. She didn't want to look at what it is. She scuffed her shoe into the nap of the carpet.

She found a cordless phone and hit the talk button. The instrument was dead, and she didn't have her cell phone. She'd have to go back downstairs to call this in . . . whatever it was. A double mutilation murder. She pushed from her mind a pile of messy questions, not the least of which was about how two strapping street thugs could have been . . .

Then, suddenly, weird things began to happen.

It must have come out of one of the bedrooms. Unseen, its odor hit her first. It was the worst wet-dog smell imaginable, an evil musk of dirt and sweat and unnamable exudations.

She turned and saw two red eyes advancing toward her. It was little more than a huge dark shape, a flash of something white and sharp, and slits of molten eyes, all revealed in a second's sweep of the weak penlight beam

There was some discontinuity of time. The thing attacked as a molasses-like goo enveloped everything, a slowness, a dreamlike slow-motion falling, a nightmare environment of some kind took over and she was fighting to move, fighting an inelastic medium that held her back; but not everything was affected. Her right hand, utterly within its own frame of reference, instantly grew a mailed gauntlet to cover it and metal feathers like wings along the side of her hand and wrist to embellish it. The Witchblade had reacted faster than she possibly could have.

The gauntlet lashed out, its metallic talons ripping and tearing.

The thing howled and staggered back.

The rest of her body caught up to the Blade's time frame. She moved back in strategic retreat, back-kicking debris out of the way. She leapt over a cocktail table and kicked in the monster's direction.

The thing howled again and swiped at the Blade as it passed. Flinders flew in all directions. The thing then circled to the right, slowly, cautiously. It had cause now to take the measure of the adversary it faced, to calculate the nature of the threat. It slunk, it crouched. It growled.

She watched it, tensed to spring into action. Her eyes now saw in the dark like an infrared camera.

It stopped. The beast's fiery eyes never wavered, never blinked.

She eased to the right, sidestepping gingerly.

It sprang forward in a rush, wickedly fast. She leapt away and kicked.

The thing grunted as it tripped over an immense

overstuffed armchair deftly slid into its path. It fell over the thing and ended up a heap on the floor behind it. It remained out of sight a few seconds. She moved off and took a stance on the opposite side of the room.

It was annoyed now. She noted that its bestial growling carried an intelligent undertone. It was as if the creature could speak but chose not to, or was contemptuous of communicating with a creature as low as the one it faced. Nevertheless its guttural sounds carried meaning. Now it was thoroughly peeved, as if a simple task had proved surprisingly troublesome. There came a sense that this female creature had been underestimated, and some blame was to be assigned for this failure of foresight. Nevertheless, the job of destroying her had to be done. And this task the creature would accomplish, without further delay. It sprang over the overturned chair and rushed again.

This time it met the full force of the Witchblade, a steely haymaker that sent it crashing against the wall.

The thing was stunned, but only momentarily. It howled out pain and immense anger as it got to its feet.

To Sara, the thing was still just a black shape in the dark. There was a suggestion of the lupine—pointed ears, long muzzle, canine incisors—but there was more to the creature. It was humanoid, it was bipedal, and it had fully prehensile forelimbs tipped with wicked claws. That much detail was visible. But its shape seemed to shift and reconfigure at times, as if it were still deciding what it wanted to be, or perhaps the best shape to assume for the task at hand.

But it was wary now. It almost sauntered to its left, moving away from the wall, side-stepping upset furniture, and from it came a sound faintly like a chuckle, a false note of nonchalance, which was instantly belied. The thing swiped at a shelf, came away with some knickknack that had miraculously survived, and threw it viciously across the room.

She dodged it easily.

It chortled and kept ambling.

She tried to keep the jumble of wreckage between her and it, watching, trying to guess its next avenue of attack, for it was only a matter of time before it came at her again. She moved off to one side, stopped, recomputed the angles, moved once more. She could see enough detail in the apartment to do this. The creature, however, was still amorphous, mostly a black-on-black enigma. It seemed to bleed into the shadows, metamorphosing and flowing, and the shadows writhed themselves in coils and swirls.

They danced this way from room to room and back again to the living area. The thing feinted, swiped at the air, shadow-boxed and threatened, but made no move to carry through an attack. It had been stung, and it was chary of launching into another foray before gaining some overwhelming advantage.

The delaying tactics were getting to Sara. When this horrific *pas de deux* had gone on for over a minute, she took a step forward, tiring of the game.

"Bring it on, puppy dog," she said.

It almost laughed. You could have called it a laugh, a deeply malevolent chuckle that carried an edge of vicious glee.

You could almost hear it say, *Worry not, hellbitch, I shall accommodate you.*

But apparently she wasn't close enough.

"Let's get it on, dude."

You are a vexing creature. What exactly is your nature?

"Guess."

The thing did not answer. It stooped, picked up a magazine stand, and threw.

She ducked. "That all you can do? It seems so petty."

It threw a trivet table in answer.

She zigged, then zagged as a big glass ashtray went sailing past. It shattered in the darkness.

The thing roared as it lifted the huge couch.

"Careful, don't get a hernia. That is, if you have any balls."

But the move was a feint. The critter simply dropped the thing and bounded over it like a gazelle, and in so doing finally caught her by surprise.

In a flash, the enigma was on top of her, slashing and tearing, and it was all she could do to fend off its blows. One miss, and she was steak tartar. But she had no options other than to keep back. Move inside, and come in range of those oversize teeth, those impossibly long and gleaming white spikes of dentition that looked more appropriate on an alligator. Viewed at close quarters, the creature was a polyglot of animal configurations—there a touch of wild bore, here a hint of *Tyrannosaurus rex*. The wolfish composite was simply an overall style.

The thing got hold of her and she had to grab its muzzle with the gauntlet, which crushed the beast's mouth together like a garlic press. The thing howled in pain, and she squeezed tighter.

They rolled across the floor, debris flying everywhere. She kicked and punched, squeezed and wrestled. The smell of it was unbearable.

The rolling and straining and howling and everything else went on for an interminable period. Plaster fell from the walls, windows shattered.

At some point, her memory of specific actions trailed off . . . another discontinuity. Then time resumed and she was on her feet and hitting the thing. She struck it again and again with all her might, summoning all the strength of the Witchblade. She took a step back, hauled off, swung and landed a horrendous blow.

The thing lurched back.

She advanced and struck again. And again, and once more. The creature keened, shrinking under a rain of blows that could have reduced an elephant to hamburger. The beast backed off and hit a wall, fell to a sitting position.

She stood looking at it, arm raised for another smash. She froze.

The thing looked at her.

"Well?" she thundered.

The creature got up, shook itself, and stalked off in a huff, grumbling.

Okay, if you're going to be nasty about it . . .

She couldn't believe it as she watched the critter shamble back into the bedroom, presumably whence it had come.

Bitch.

The door slammed.

Sara bounded over to the door and threw it open. She wasn't surprised to find that the creature was gone.

Some semblance of mundane reality resumed. She finally found a light switch and flicked it on. Her Witchblade accoutrements had withdrawn back into the bracelet, leaving her in tattered clothing.

The place was . . . indescribable. Splinters of wood, scraps of paper, potsherds, blood, body parts—almost nothing in the room was in one piece save the sofa. She didn't want to inventory body bits. Not her job. She knew what had happened to Anton and Sergei. If indeed the parts added up to Anton and Sergei. She saw a severed head in a far corner. She did not want to identify it. Leave it to the forensic examiner.

The door flew open and two uniformed officers rushed in. They stopped in their tracks and gaped. She turned and regarded them, feeling rather odd.

One of them said, "What in the name of all that's holy . . . ?"

She tried to smile. "Uh, I can explain. . . ."

CHAPTER

TWELVE

The study of Kenneth Irons was a study in itself, lavish with *objets d'art* and all manner of fine things. Busts of the legendary crowned the bookcases, deistic statues posed in corners. Egyptian antiquities occupied prominent places, the plunder of ransacked tombs lending an ancient resplendence. The room boasted many Oriental pieces as well.

Two Asian gentlemen were ushered in and seated.

"Good evening," said Irons as he seated himself across the lacquered table.

The two men nodded.

"Mr. Fong," he said to the one on his right. "Mr. Kitisawa," to the other. "The Triad and the Yakusa, together at last."

The two Asian men looked at each other and grunted.

"We do business all the time," said Kitisawa.

"Though at times we do compete," Fong said.

"No doubt," Irons said. "I will leave it to you to coordinate your activities with Asian organizations of other ethnic flavors: Viet, Thai, Indonesian, etcetera.

There really is quite an assortment these days. Mr. Fong, your operations center in Hong Kong and extend to San Francisco?"

"Yes."

"Mr. Kitisawa. Tokyo and Los Angeles, is it?"

"Quite so."

"And you both have networks here in the States, of course. I could have called a general conference, but this is more economical. Between the two of you, you control the vast, vast Pacific Rim."

"There is no problem about coordination," Mr. Fong said. "I should not worry, Mr. Irons."

"I rarely do. Gentlemen, by reputation, I know you to be modern-minded, forward-looking leaders. You know what the new spheres of activity encompass, what they entail. And, of course, the key is the computer and the infinite worldwide web it spins."

"Like a steel spider," Kitisawa said.

"One of silicon?" Fong ventured.

Kitisawa smiled.

"They say," Irons went on, "that no one can control the web. I think they are wrong."

Both his guests grinned broadly.

"I need you gentlemen to help me tame it. You need my . . . considerable resources."

"Yes, indeed," Fong replied.

"Quite so," Kitisawa agreed.

"Together I think we can impose some order on the chaos. I don't like wild, anarchic things. I like to control them. For instance, stock markets are wild, anarchic things."

Both men nodded.

"We are entering an entirely new era of world finance.

I can infuse your organizations with seed money that will reap not billions, but *trillions,* in return. You will cut yourself a piece of that. A large piece. I can afford to be generous. I'm interested more in control than in money. In fact, I have other interests entirely. But they are my private concern."

"We won't inquire," Kitisawa said.

"Thank you, gentlemen. My subordinates will contact you with details."

The two men across from Irons sat back, ready perhaps for a nice chat. Tea?

"That is all," Irons said.

The two sat up abruptly. They rose and bowed, then left the room.

Irons leaned back and irreverently put his feet up on the immaculately polished table.

He laughed.

"Okay, let's go over this again," Seltzer was saying. "You were conducting an undercover operation on your own . . ."

"Not exactly," Sara told him.

The room was crowded. At least a dozen crime scene investigators swarmed through the place, swabbing and gathering, scooping and bagging.

"Not exactly. Now, you know these guys. You went to a concert with them last night."

"With their boss, really."

"With their boss, a known organized crime figure."

"Yes."

"And you went out with this criminal for what reason, again?"

"To gather intelligence on his operations."

"On your own hook."

"On my own hook," Sara informed him.

"And you came up here, broke in . . ."

"Had the keys."

"Which you confiscated from the bartender, who, by the way . . ."

"He was there all night. He served me three drinks."

"And now no one's ever heard of him."

"Right. There's a different bartender down there now. He must have reported on duty when I came upstairs."

"But the new guy never heard of this other bartender. The baby-faced kid."

"That's what he says."

"So you have nothing and no one to back up your story."

"It's not a story," Sara told him. "It's a preliminary oral report."

"Yeah. Yeah."

"Seltzer!"

Sara and Seltzer turned toward the door as Joe Siry stormed in. He was about to say something when he caught sight of the carnage.

"Jesus Christ!" Appalled, he scanned the room with disgust. "What in God's green earth went on here?"

"We don't know," Seltzer said. "Detective Pezzini might, but she's not saying."

"Why do you assume she knows anything? Didn't she phone this in?"

"No," Seltzer said. "Patrons downstairs heard a ruckus upstairs and called 911. The local precinct answered the call. The officers who responded found your detective here, dressed like this." He gestured at her torn clothing.

"You off-duty?" Siry asked her.

"Yes," Sara said.

Siry turned back to Seltzer. "Then what's the problem?"

"The problem," Seltzer began, "is that no one else was in the apartment. No one saw anyone go down the back stairs to the bar, and the front entrance, which you get to via stairs on the other side of that door, is deadbolted from the inside. She sat in the bar all evening and even *she* says no one came down those back stairs. She was the only one seen in this apartment all night. No other way in or out."

Siry had wandered over to a shattered window and looked down. "That so?"

"There's reason to believe," Seltzer went on, "that the window was broken just before the officers arrived. They got here fast. They were cruising the neighborhood."

"Yeah? Okay, so you think my detective did all this?"

"I don't have any opinion. She says she found the place this way."

Siry whirled and roared, *"Then why the hell don't you believe her?"*

"I think I've outlined why there are some questions," Seltzer said mildly.

"The ruckus they heard," Sara put in, "happened after I went up."

"What happened when you went up?"

"I was attacked."

"Who did it?"

"Don't know, Cap. The apartment was dark."

"You fought this guy?"

"Uh . . . yeah."

"And what happened?"

"He got away. Ran into a bedroom and I guess went

out a window." She inclined her head toward Seltzer. "So much for the 'no other way out' theory."

"You didn't pursue?"

"As I said, Cap, it was dark. His eyes must have adapted. I was blind."

Siry nodded. "Uh-huh, uh-huh. Okay. Well, that explains that. I guess."

"We'll have to check the neighborhood for any sightings of somebody coming out that window," Seltzer said. "As I mentioned, there are questions, that's all. Plenty of them, including the question of how the guy could have jumped two stories onto concrete."

"Lots of second-story men can jump two stories," Siry said. "What's so hard to understand?"

Seltzer smiled unctuously. "I like a commanding officer who backs his men to the hilt. Loyalty is a two-way street. Admirable. Well, listen. I have to run, and the techs have to do their job. I'd like to see the report as soon as you can get it to me, Detective Pezzini."

"You'll get it," Siry said.

Seltzer shrugged amiably. "Fine." He turned and exited via the back stairs.

Siry walked slowly toward Sara. He crunched something underfoot, stopped, looked down, and kicked. A shard of china went skittering.

"Disturbing evidence?" Sara asked.

"This isn't evidence. This is a goddamn disaster."

"Sorry for another screw-up. Sorry I let him get away."

"What could you do? It was dark. You said."

"Yeah, I said that."

"Is it true?"

"It's true it was dark. It's also true that I don't know what the hell it was I tussled with. It was something

112

weird, and yet another thing I can't really explain. Nor do I have an explanation for this mess. Except to say that the strange thing I encountered must have done it. Beyond that, I'll be novelizing my report again."

Siry laughed mirthlessly.

"Jesus H. Christ!"

They both turned to see Jake McCarthy standing at the back door. His jaw was hanging.

"Excuse the mess," Sara said. "We didn't have time to clean today."

"My God," Jake breathed. He extended his arms helplessly. "What . . . ?"

"Don't ask," Sara said. "What's even worse," she added to Siry, "is that I don't have an explanation for why no one heard anything before I went up. Because if the perp was hanging around, that sort of implies he'd just done it, and I walked in just after. But how did he do this butcher job without making a sound?"

"I see what you mean," Siry said. "That is a problem. You have any solutions?"

"Not at the moment." Sara sighed, shaking her head.

"Got any idea about a motive?" Siry asked.

"Nope. I *do* know that these two guys did the hit on Ashkenazi."

"How? I mean, how do you know?"

"Because I was out with them, and they disappeared at just the right time."

"You were out with their boss. Kontra."

"Yeah, and they were his bodyguards, his muscle. They left the concert about forty-five minutes before the hit went down. The victim was probably the guy who put out the contract on Kontra—the hit that failed."

"So Kontra's good for the hit," Siry said.

"Sure."

"So we can go to a judge and get a warrant. Easy."

Sara frowned and looked at the floor.

"Easy," Siry repeated. "Right?"

Sara started moving toward the door. "See you, Cap."

"Yeah, good night, Sara. Thanks. Oh, by the way . . ."

She stopped.

"You're to stay away from organized crime cases. I don't want you near anything resembling a mob-related incident. Leave it to the Task Force and the feds. And that's an order."

"Sure," she said in a small voice.

THIRTEEN

Mrs. Kontra?"

A dried husk of a face appeared in the crack between door and jamb.

"Who are you?

Sara held up her badge. "New York Police Department, ma'am. Some questions?"

"Who are you?"

As if the question had never been answered. Sara tried again. "NYPD? Police? We have some questions for Mr. Kontra."

"Who?"

"Mr. Lazlo Kontra. He lives here." That was not a question.

"No one lives here but me."

"We've talked to the super. We know who pays rent here."

"Go away, devil woman."

"Mrs. Kontra . . . if that's who you are."

"I'm his grandmother."

"Okay. Your grandson's name isn't on the lease, but he

lives here, full time. At least that's what the landlord will admit. Your grandson pays the rent. Do you live here, too?"

The old woman widened the door and looked at Sara for a long moment. "Come in. I want to see you."

"Uh . . . sure." *And what Bela Lugosi movie did you walk out of, Madame Ouspenskaya?*

Sara's idle thought got pushed aside as she entered what was a perfectly conventional apartment. The only thing Slavic about it (were Romanians Slavs?) was a faint odor of cabbage.

"Sit."

Sara sat in an easy chair with a flower-print slipcover. Very Wal-Mart. She watched the old woman disappear into the kitchen.

The babushka-headed woman returned shortly with a glass and a bottle. She sat the glass on the coffee table and poured out about two fingers of an amber liquid.

"Tuica," she said. "Plum brandy."

Ah, a traditional Romanian drink? It sounded good. Should she throw it down or mutter the usual dodge about being on duty? Well, she wasn't officially on duty, was she?

To hell with it. She lifted the glass and took the shot in one gulp. It was thick, sweet, and damn good. "Very nice. Thank you."

The woman sat on the matching sofa. She was smiling oddly.

"Where is Lazlo?" Sara asked.

The old woman shrugged. "He does not tell me where he go."

"My files say he has a farm upstate. Someone else owns it, but like this apartment, he has complete use of the place. But he makes the mortgage payments on the farm. Is that where he is?"

"I never go there."

"Are you saying it's true? That he does visit this farm now and then?"

"We were all farmers in the old country. Nothing else to do."

"I see. How often does he go there?"

"He doesn't tell me his business."

"And he has a lot of businesses. Right?"

The old woman shrugged.

Sara sat back. "You wanted to see me, you said."

"You are beautiful girl."

"Thank you, Mrs. . . . Madame Kontra?"

"I am Lazlo's father's mother. He calls me Baba. You can call me Baba, too."

"Baba, I need to talk to your grandson. He did a nasty thing to me."

The old woman raised her eyebrows. "He touched you?"

"I'm not talking about anything . . ." Sara sat up and unconsciously arranged her blue-jeaned legs more primly. More ladylike? Boy, this was going to be a hard interview. "He wasn't completely honest with me, Baba. He compromised me. Uh, I don't mean . . ."

"You are a strange one. That bracelet on your wrist."

Sara glanced at the Witchblade. "This? What about it?"

"It is old, very old."

"Yes, that's true. How did you know?"

"I don't know much. I am stupid old woman. But I can

117

see things. I see fire around this bracelet. Ghost fire. It is from a far place, somewhere men cannot reach. It is from hell, but it is not the devil's hell. It . . ."

Sara waited.

The old woman looked off. "I don't know," she said simply.

"Do you do magic?" Sara asked.

"I know some magic. I protect my grandson. He is in danger. He has enemies. He always has enemies. He needs protection by the spirits."

"Which spirits?"

"The good spirits. Not like the colored boy's."

Sara did a take. "What colored boy?"

"The colored boy, works for Lazlo. I see him here once. He is one of Lazlo's men, but not like the two big ones. He is like an owl. Very, very smart."

"And he does magic?"

"As black as his skin." Baba thought about it for a moment. "His skin is not so dark, actually. But you know what I mean."

"Have you talked with him about doing magic?"

"No. I never talk with him."

"I see. But you know he does magic."

"I see the light around him. Like you."

"Oh, I understand. You simply . . . intuited . . . uh, you saw the light."

"Yes. The magic light. He does evil magic. Sometimes. I don't think he is evil. He is just a boy, really. But he does dangerous things."

"There's some danger in using this evil magic?"

"Oh, my God, yes. Danger. The things, they come from Hell, and they do what you want, but then . . . ah, but then . . ." Baba chuckled.

"So this black person . . . what's his name?"

"I don't know."

"It would help if I had his name."

"People don't tell me their names. I mind my own business."

"I see. Baba, do you know what kind of business your grandson is in?"

"Oil. He has men drive oil truck."

"Yes. Did you know . . ." Sara turned and looked out the window. This was useless. She rose and smiled at Baba. "Thank you, Madame Kontra. Baba."

"Beautiful girl. Why do you dress like farm worker?"

"I've always been a tomboy."

"What is that? Why don't you wear a dress? You would look so pretty in nice dress."

"Sometimes I do."

"All the time, in Romania, they make women dress like men. The Communists liked that. I told them, I will work like dog, but I won't dress like man. That is wrong."

"Sure. Listen, thank you very much for talking to me. I'll let myself out."

The old woman got to her feet. She seemed to have life in her, for all that her skin looked like the Dead Sea Scrolls. "You are wanted by many spirits."

Sara looked over her shoulder as she advanced toward the door. "That so? By whom, exactly?"

"Strange spirits. I do not know them."

"Good or evil?" Sara asked as she opened the door.

"I don't know. I would tell you if I knew. I like you. You would make my grandson good wife if this one dies. Good wife."

"Uh . . . thank you. I think."

She went out and eased the door shut.

* * *

Sara stood at her desk, which was a mess. As usual. It was piled with printouts, reports, memos, bulletins, and endless other species of paperwork.

"Why *can't* you tell me?" she demanded.

She pressed the phone tighter to her ear, trying to block out the sound of the radio that someone insisted on playing full blast in his office. "What do you mean, 'need-to-know basis'? What's that supposed to mean? Are we talking about classified secrets, here?"

Jake McCarthy walked into the squad room with two civilians in tow, a middle-aged couple. Both were well-dressed and looked well-to-do. He saw that Sara was on the phone. "This is Detective Pezzini. She might be able to help you. She was the arresting officer."

The man said, "Thank you."

Jake exited. Sara was looking at the visitors out of the corner of one eye. "Okay. Yeah. Yeah. If that's how it is." She hung up and turned to face them. "Can I help you?"

"Yes," the man said. "You were the officer who was present when my son died?"

"Your son?"

"I'm Ross Bromley. Charles Bromley was my son. Charles Morton Bromley, the Second? He was named after his grandfather."

Sara started. "Oh. Oh, yes. I knew him by another name."

"Yes. 'Kool Whip,' I believe." Bromley sighed. "He ... Charles lived on the street, didn't he? At least, he ended up there. He graduated from college, did you know that?"

"I wasn't aware."

"He studied art. He was quite a good sculptor, so they tell me."

"I see."

"Yes, he studied it in school. He started with painting but he decided it was—what was his phrase?—an 'effete art form.' He liked to work in metal. He had a show. Oh, this was quite a while ago."

"A show," Sara said. "Sculpture."

"Quite a while ago. Ten years. He was very young. And then he . . ."

"He got into drugs," the mother said.

"And he sort of fell apart. What we wanted to ask—"

"I'm very sorry," Sara blurted. "It was a tragic thing, your son's death."

"Thank you," Bromley said. "We wanted to know if he said anything before he threw himself off the balcony."

"Threw himself?"

"Well, that's what the letter from the police department said. It made it sound like suicide. That he threw himself off and killed himself."

"Oh. It wasn't quite like that. He fell. It was an accident."

"Well, the letter was really very unclear about that. It used the word accident, but the way it described what happened . . ."

"We just couldn't believe it," the mother said. "Not our Charlie. He was so full of life. When he was a boy . . ."

"We're not going to sue," the father said sternly. "We wanted to tell you that. Our society is being torn apart by litigation. Entirely too much legalistic folderol. We realize that Charles was in part culpable. We support the police."

"But we wanted to know if he said anything before he died," the mother said. "And he died so horribly. We want to know if he suffered."

"I don't think he did," Sara said evenly. "It was over

very quickly. He didn't have time to say anything. The whole thing was an unfortunate accident. I'm truly very sorry, Mr. and Mrs. Bromley."

"Thank you," the father said. "Uh, your name again? I'm sorry."

"Sara Pezzini."

"Thank you, Officer Pezzini," the mom said. "Can I ask exactly how you came to know our son?"

"He . . . worked with us. He helped us out on occasion. With tips, information."

"Oh, so he helped the police?" Mrs. Bromley asked.

"Yes, he did."

She smiled. "We didn't know that. He actually helped the police department?"

"He did a good job. I also saw his sculpture. He was very talented."

"He was," the mother said, glowing inside. A single tear had welled up, and it hung at the corner of her eye like a tiny diamond. "He was so talented."

When they left, Sara felt as if she had shrunk a few inches during the conversation.

She got back on the phone.

"One bam!"

"Two crack!"

These Chinese played Mah Jongg with a vengeance. Fast, and tiles face down, announced once and then hidden for the rest of the hand. Not American style, where they lie face up. You had to have a good memory and keep your ears open. And lots of money to get a seat at the table. At a buck a point, this was no game for amateurs.

Merlin looked at his tiles. He was waiting for one tile, a white dragon. He had a red and green. A white would give him a rare hand, one worth many points. Dragons were not often discarded, but sometimes a player had no choice but to discard, if he had only one and no match.

Chen was smiling at him. "You haven't put up any tiles? You must be working on something, or trying for a completely hidden hand."

"I like to play it close to the vest," Merlin said.

"I like the way you play," Chen said, picking up a tile. "You play fast. Not like most Americans."

"I'm having trouble keeping up with you guys. Thanks for sticking to English most of the time."

"Least we can do. This is a friendly game. As I said, I think you'll enjoy working with us. You're very talented and knowledgeable. We can make a lot of money in the east. Hong Kong is still a wide-open city."

"I'm sure. What wind are we on?"

"North. This is the last hand, Merlin."

"Ah. Okay, thanks. Is it my turn?"

"Yes."

Merlin took a tile from the Wall, looked at it, and set it down. "Six bamboo."

"Got it," the player to Merlin's right announced. He took the tile and matched it up with two more of its like on his rack. The triplet was worth only two points, but it was good towards Mah Jongg.

"I hear," Merlin said, "that the mainland government is being very cooperative with business. They don't want to kill the goose, so to speak."

"That is completely right. We have many contacts in Peking. Most people don't think that would be the case."

"Seems natural to me," Merlin said.

"You have no problem with that, then?" Chen asked.

"Not in the least. I like the sound of your money."

"You'll find us much more generous than our Russian colleagues."

"They're pretty tight with a ruble. Or a dollar, I should say."

"Then we have a deal?" Chen asked.

"White dragon," said the player in the East position, and put down a tile. Merlin grabbed it. There was no dragon on the white tile; just a black border. A white dragon is invisible in snow.

"Mah Jongg!" Merlin peeled.

"Very good!" Chen said amiably.

Merlin put up his tiles.

Chen's jaw dropped. "Oh, my God."

Merlin laid out one of each dragon, one of each wind, one each of suit in terminals.

"Fourteen Noble Scholars!" Chen exclaimed in genuine amazement. "I've seen that hand only one other time in my life!"

"I was dealt most of it," Merlin said with pride. "I had to draw only three tiles, but had to wait forever for that last dragon."

"Amazing," Chen said. "Well, that's a limit hand. And limit for this club is a thousand points. You've just won three thousand dollars. Thank Confucius you weren't East. You would have cleaned us out."

CHAPTER

FOURTEEN

As she drove farther out into the countryside, Sara couldn't get some thoughts out of her mind. The general way the department handled informants sometimes bothered her. How many times had her division used the squeeze, threatening an informant with an indictment unless he or she cooperated? Sometimes the informant had to place his life on the line, risk retaliation, retribution. A few times such an informant had paid with his life. The squeeze was an oft-used tool of the district attorney's office, with the police implementing.

She had always hated it. For all that informants were usually low-life scum, they had rights, too. She felt a general, all-purpose guilt over Charlie Bromley's death. The specifics didn't apply. She hadn't squeezed him, but she could not get shed of doubts about the ethics of standard police tactics.

It was a cold day, the first really cold day of fall. Clouds drifted like smoke across a white sky broken only by bare trees. She urged the little subcompact along a two-lane road, hayfields at either shoulder. She was far into Connecticut, and if she drove half an hour more, she'd be in Massachusetts.

Obeying directions given at a convenience store a few miles back, she bore left at the next intersection and took a narrow oil-and-gravel road. She was looking for a small farm owned by a family named Paunescu. That was the name on the list of Kontra's "Known Associates (Possible Non-Combatants)." People he did business with but were not soldiers in the Organizatiya. The Paunescu family lived on the farm, but did not own it. They lived rent free; nevertheless, they were virtual tenants. They did whatever Kontra needed of them. Kontra's name was not to be found on the deed or any legal title to the land, but he was lord of every acre. The Paunescus were, in effect, his serfs.

At least that was her theory. And it was a pretty good theory. These absentee-owner farms, the fiefdoms of an ethnic rainbow of gangs, lay all over the tri-state area. They served various purposes: hideouts, storage facilities, and potter's fields for the dead bodies of people who would never be seen again by kith or kin.

Thank God she knew someone in the district attorney's office. Guy who'd been wanting to date her for years. She hoped she didn't have to return the favor someday. He was nice, but hardly her type. Another reason to feel guilty.

The Paunescus' farm had been on that list, and its location. She was taking an awful chance.

Siry would kill her if he found out. She knew he would eventually. She wondered if she subconsciously liked it when she ran afoul of him, if she relished the attention that got her. The daddy's-little-girl syndrome again?

She pushed it from her mind.

Besides, she'd missed the dirt road she was looking for. She hit the brakes and turned around. As she did, a few lone snowflakes drifted past the windshield. This early? Then she glanced at the date on her watch and realized how much of the month had melted away. Winter was almost here.

She saw now that she'd driven past a narrow dirt road that debouched onto the pavement behind some tall weeds. The lone sentinel of a mailbox stood beside it. The lettering read PAUNESCU. She turned in.

The road was rutty but passable. Gravel bounced off the undercarriage. The road wound through tall trees interspersed with brambles of brown underbrush. Tufts of green appeared here and there, last remnants of summer making a stand, and here and there branches hung festooned with colorful fall foliage.

A single red leaf fluttered to the hood and blew off.

Fog began to gather. Fast, as if on cue, it coalesced and transformed crisp air to thick, heavy soup. She slowed the car. A farmhouse appeared ahead, something behind it. Another house, or a barn? It was bigger than the main house. Or the rear house was the main house.

She pulled up to the end of the driveway and parked beside an aging foreign pickup. She got out. The place, of dirty white siding with faded blue shutters, was a little run down, but looked comfortable in a squalid kind of way. This was no prosperous farm, if farm it really was. Junk littered a side yard. She looked it over. The obligatory rusting pickup with attendant old refrigerators.

She mounted the rickety porch and knocked on the door. After some activity inside, it opened, and a man in his forties poked his head out.

"Yes?"

"Mr. Paunescu?"

"You probably want my father. He owns the place. He's not well. Can I help you?"

"Is Mr. Kontra here?"

The man, rather sallow-faced and thin, acquired a blank look. "Who?"

"Is that his house in the back?"

"Place has been empty for years," he said.

"Does your father own it?"

"Yes."

"Really? And you live in this place?"

"It's mainly for hunters. Weekenders, that sort of thing. My dad rents it out. Who may I ask are you?"

"I'm a New York City police officer, looking for Mr. Lazlo Kontra. Do you know him?"

"I've heard of him."

"Is he a friend of your father's?"

"Not sure."

"Could he be currently renting the back place?"

"I don't think anyone's rented the back place for a while. I haven't seen a car parked there. My father doesn't tell me his business. Sorry."

"You live here and don't know if anyone's renting the place?"

"Haven't been back there for a while."

"You do live here?" Sara asked.

"Yes, with my parents. They're getting old, and I take care of the place, more or less. Look, what's this all about, if I can ask?"

"I'm simply looking for him. Had trouble getting in touch with him lately."

His eyebrows drew together suspiciously. "Do you have a search warrant?"

"This isn't an official visit. I'm a friend of his."

"Really? Oh. Well, you're asking a lot of questions. Only my father can answer, and he's sleeping. He shouldn't be disturbed. As I said, he's sick. His heart."

"Is your mother here?"

"No. She's visiting relatives. Sorry. I'll tell my father you dropped by."

"Mind if I look the place over?"

"Uh . . ."

"I was thinking about renting a place in the country. For weekends."

The man was reluctant, but didn't want to appear evasive. "I guess you can look around."

"Thanks."

He poked his head out the door. "Weather's turning bad. Looks like snow."

"Yeah, it's starting to come down. I'll just look the place over and leave. Sorry to bother you."

"Okay."

She walked around the back of the place. More junk, but it had an ordered look to it. A large vegetable garden lay on the outskirts of a neglected lawn. A few hardy plants still grew in it, onions and such.

The house in back was farther away than she'd first thought. It stood on a rise that sloped away rapidly to deep woods. She stuck to the trees as she walked around the right side. There was a vehicle parked behind the house, a black late-model SUV.

The house was one of those modern log constructions, but was hardly a cabin. It looked to have at least ten rooms, all on one floor. A huge fieldstone chimney dominated the rear. A big deck patio ran off sliding glass doors and massive windows at the other end of the house.

She sneaked up on a small back window and looked in. The lights were on inside a bedroom that looked to have been converted to an office. A young black man sat at a compact workstation typing on a desktop computer. She'd never seen the young man before, but could guess who he was. Another man, a husky type with the look of a street hood, sat in an easy chair on the other side of the room reading a slick men's magazine. He had the centerfold out and was studying it intently.

She peeked in. Almost instantly, the black man turned and saw her. He made no reaction other than to shift his eyes to the zine-reading gunsel. Then he looked at her again, at first quizzical, then pleading, his eyebrows communicating something. What was he trying to say? To Sara it looked as though he were warning, *Watch out*.

Sara flattened herself against the log exterior.

Wait. This was no good. She wasn't going to break into the place. This wasn't a raid. Couldn't be. She didn't have authorization to be here, let alone a warrant. This was another jurisdiction entirely. Hell, this was another state.

When in doubt, launch an all-out frontal assault.

She walked around the building, mounted the spacious porch, and knocked at the front door. As she did, snow began to fall in earnest.

The door stayed shut. She gave it at least a minute, then knocked again.

The door opened. And there stood the man who'd been reading the girly zine. "Come in, Detective."

"I don't believe I've had the pleasure," Sara said as she stepped into a big foyer. She never seen a log cabin with a foyer before.

"Vladimir," he said.

"You work for Mr. Kontra?"

"Yes. He will see you. Come this way, please."

Vladimir led the way out of the foyer and straight into a huge room with an imposing fireplace, to the right of which began a sweeping panorama of windows.

Kontra stood in the corner, smiling at her.

"What a surprise," he said.

"Was in the neighborhood, thought I'd drop in," Sara said.

"I'm glad you did. I suppose you want to talk to me."

"I'm really pissed off at you."

Kontra nodded understandingly. "I see. I see. Well, I don't blame you. It was unfortunate, the way it looked."

"That way what looked?"

"That I used you as alibi."

"Ah, that occurred to you," Sara said brightly.

"Yes. Yes, it looked that way, but it isn't true. Ashkenazi . . . well, I heard about him. He was my enemy. He hates me from way back. In Moscow. He thinks I killed his brother. He was thief, and his brother, too. His brother was killed in prison, and he blames me."

"You didn't strangle him?"

Kontra's right eyebrow lifted slightly. "How did you hear this accusation?"

"These things get around."

"But this happened in Russia long time ago. Please sit."

Sara took a seat on one of the plaid couches. "So it happened?"

"I misspoke. It *didn't* happen in Russia, long time ago, my killing him. But he died in prison. That happened."

"Ashkenazi was your enemy, but you didn't have him killed?"

"No."

"You didn't send Anton and Sergei to shoot him with a
.22 caliber pistol?"

"No."

"But now Anton and Sergei are dead."

"Yes. And you were there."

Sara crossed her long legs. "You have ways of getting
information, too."

"Absolutely," Kontra said. "You were there. Not only
that, you might have killed them."

"Really. You think that."

"Baba thinks that, too."

"So we each suspect the other of murder."

"Looks that way. I'm wondering why you come here."

"I'm wondering, too," Sara said. "Maybe it's because I
have no other way of solving this case."

"What case are you solving, Ashkenazi?"

"Maybe. You wiseguy cases are all the same. It's not so
much solving the case as getting court evidence that
won't disappear or end up dead. And killing Anton and
Sergei is a good way of getting rid of evidence."

Kontra said, "You want a drink?"

"No thanks."

"Why did you come here? What do you think you will
find?"

"I don't know. But I wonder what we'd find if we dug
around."

Kontra shrugged. "Dirt. This is farm, you know."

"You never know what you might find in the dirt."

Kontra looked off. "There are roads, they run near the
property. Anybody can stop, dig, bury something."

"You know where all the bodies are buried."

Kontra laughed. "Where do you think you will start?
There are four hundred acres."

"Be interesting to see what we can dig up."

"Have a good time."

Vladimir came in and said something in Russian to Kontra. Kontra expressed annoyance and gave an order. Vladimir nodded and left in a hurry.

"What was that all about?" Sara asked.

"Nothing."

"Did your guest take a hike?"

"Guest?"

"The black kid. Your hacker."

"Hacker?" Kontra echoed.

"Computer whiz. Techno-nerd."

"You know, American slang is still mystery to me sometimes. There is so much of it. Russian slang has lots, too. But I think I hear new American slang every day."

"Romanian have slang?"

"Not so much. More dialect, you call it."

"He seems to be here against his will," Sara told him. "He been giving you trouble?"

"No trouble."

"Are you going to sic the werewolf on him?"

"What nonsense do you speak now? Werewolf. What do you think, you are in movie?"

"I think that's what did in Anton and Sergei."

Kontra frowned dyspeptically. "Now you are making me sick. You accuse some werewolf, but you did it."

"What in the world makes you think that? Did Baba give you that idea?"

"She says nothing about werewolf. She says you are devil woman."

"I don't know, Lazlo. Romania, werewolves. Kind of go together."

"Do you think we are magicians? Witches, sorcerers? Romanians are just people. You shouldn't believe Hollywood."

"I don't. But I know I didn't tear Anton and Sergei apart. I have no motive. I'm a police . . . person." Sara cringed inwardly.

Kontra guffawed. "You think that makes you holy? I made inquiries into your department. You are far from holy person. You are soon to be indicted."

Sara looked at him calmly. But her stomach twisted. "Your sources aren't very accurate."

"We'll see. It is funny. You come here, you charge me with killing stupid thief Ashkenazi. Mob hit, you say. But you are charged with being mob hit man."

"Hit person. The silly things some people say."

"Yes. Like you will dig for bodies here. You won't find anything. And who will listen when district attorney indicts you? No one."

"I'm still going to come here and dig."

"Not today?" Kontra leaned forward. "You don't have warrant?"

"Not today. But I'll be back."

"You don't have warrant? You just come up here to talk?"

"Pretty much. Just to let you know that I'm on to you."

It sounded lame even to Sara. But she wasn't about to let her face show it.

"Oh," Kontra said quietly, nodding. "That's nice."

Sara rose. "I'm taking the kid."

"What?"

"The hacker kid. I believe he's here under duress. I'm taking him back to New York, if he wants to go."

Kontra rose and shrugged expansively. "He's not here."

"I saw him through the window."

"He left. He's not prisoner. You are making a mistake."

"He ran off, probably. Didn't you send Vladimir after him?"

"I sent Vladimir on errand."

"I'll bet."

Sara drew her pistol. Kontra laughed at it.

"You are silly thing. What do you think you will do?"

"Just in case Vladimir gives me trouble."

"You are not in New York. This is state of Connecticut. You have no business up here."

"Connecticut is New York's bedroom. So long, Laz."

Sara walked to the sliding glass door and yanked it open. It slid with alarming ease and thumped violently against the opposite jamb.

"Careful!" Kontra yelled.

"Sorry."

"Crazy woman."

Snow already covered the yard. It was a thick, wet, early snow, the kind that slops down in late October and tries to get a head start on Christmas. But it never works. It melts almost instantly and makes a fool of itself.

Just like Sara now. She struck out into the yard and got to the woods in about fifty quick paces.

The woods were snowy, dark, and deep, but Sara had no promises to keep, and she hoped the kid hadn't run miles into the forest. She found Vladimir's tracks easy enough. She was no woodsman, but the guy had big feet and the snow had just fallen minutes before. A blind man could have seen where he'd lit off after the kid.

The kid. Actually, he could have been in his late thirties. "Baby-faced kid," though, was the part he looked. Maybe it was his nerdly quality. Nerdish?

A shot, followed by three more in rapid succession. An eight-millimeter semiautomatic, for sure. The sound was a muffled popping that somehow hurt the ears.

Sara cut to her left. She wanted to see what Vladimir was shooting at without getting in the line of fire. She loped on into the woods, hearing some commotion off to her right and up ahead.

The snowfall was thinner here because of the trees, but the fog was gathering. It was getting harder to see. She heard something, though. Something moving through the trees. Branches were snapping like toothpicks. It was big. Very big. And strong. She had no idea what it was or exactly where it was.

More pops. Same gun, it sounded like. Vladimir was shooting at the thing, whatever it was, and he was retreating.

Something in the woods suddenly flashed and burned. The sound was like a huge blowtorch.

Sara thought that was strange. A huge blowtorch in the woods. One that moved. Something was moving up ahead, sliding through the trees and snapping branches. She couldn't see anything definite, though. All she saw was a moving white-on-white blur.

She heard a man scream. Sara stopped momentarily, then jumped to her right. She had found a deer trail, a narrow path, and ran along it toward the commotion.

Before long something very strange came along the trail the other way, running spastically. A burning man. A man on fire, his head and entire body wreathed in flames, his hair a torch.

He was screaming in pain and fear. Sara stopped and let him come at her.

He was screaming in Russian. It was Vladimir, and he

was burning to death. Sara kicked at his ankle as he passed and he went sprawling into the snow. She used her foot again to flip him over.

"Roll roll, roll!" she yelled.

He did his best, flopping over in the snow. The flames wouldn't go out so she grabbed him and rolled him, again and again until his clothes were smoking but no longer on fire.

His face was mostly carbonized, his hair burned away. He groaned and his eyes rolled up white.

"Vladimir?" she said.

He rallied to consciousness briefly, then slipped away again.

FIFTEEN

She tried to do what she could, but Vladimir was never going to get up again. She knelt there by him, a little stunned and mystified.

She got up. Vladimir was charred almost beyond recognition, but still had some life in him. She could only call for paramedics. Surely they had paramedics in this county. She got out her cell phone and hit the call button.

No service. She'd have to go back to the house. She didn't want to, but however Vladimir had conducted his life, whatever he had done in the service of some crime lord, he was still deserving of help, and she would not let him die without a call for medical aid. It was her duty as a police officer. But she had to get back first.

Which way? Simple, follow her own tracks. But the fog grew soupier as she walked and somehow she lost her own tracks. She walked on in the only direction the house could have been, or so she thought. She tramped down a shallow depression and up again.

The big log house wasn't where it should have been.

She was lost, and the fog was congealing into gaspacho;

tree trunks looked like utility poles on a London street. She could see almost nothing else. Again, though, she could hear something. It sounded familiar: slavering and gibbering, with undertones of both menace and glee.

The werewolf was now stalking her.

The fire for Vladimir; for her, getting torn apart in a rustic setting. How quaint, how positively quaint. She began to run. The snow was not yet deep, and she managed a good pace.

She ran for a good five minutes, crossing tracks at right angles twice. At least she was staying in the same general area. She ran through a patch of still-smoking woods where all the snow had melted. Tree trunks smoldered. That had been one powerful blast. More than enough to toast Vladimir.

She took a hard right, the lupine gibbering and slavering still at her heels. The thing could move fast, at least as fast as she could run. And she was now running with all her might.

The thing was gaining. Its insane chortling came closer and closer. She strained to get some distance between her and it.

The inevitable trip and fall.

She had seen it in countless movies. A female runs from the monster; she trips and falls, automatically. A movie trope if there ever was one. The chick can't get three steps before—whoopsy daisy.

And neither could she. Her right foot hit an especially slippery patch of snow, whipped out sideways, and sent her tumbling. She rolled three times and ended up sitting. The werebeast ran full tilt right at her.

She raised her arms to block a lunge for the throat.

Out of the way, bitchface.

The shaggy creature leapt over her and continued running.

Astounded, she got to her feet and followed it. Very soon she came out of the woods, into the yard, and she saw the critter lope across the garden, mindless of the onions and cauliflower, cross the lawn, bound across the deck, and throw the glass door open. The furry thing moved like nothing she had ever seen.

She heard Kontra scream.

Breaking into a dead run, she heard him begin to scream again, a horrible truncated exclamation of terror that terminated in a gurgle.

When she found him on the other side of the couch, there was less to do for him than for Vladimir. His throat was missing and a river of blood was flowing across the beige carpet. The beast was nowhere in sight. As if it had evaporated.

"Lazlo?" she said feebly. He could not answer. She fumbled with the cell phone, then remembered it was useless.

The Paunescu son barged in as she was dialing the house phone. He caught sight of Kontra's body and froze. Then he fixed Sara in a horrified stare. He turned and ran out of the house like a horse from a burning barn.

She hung up the phone, deciding she did not want to deal with Connecticut authorities. She hadn't identified herself to Paunescu. Who's to say she'd been here at all?

She did not want to be put into the position of explaining the unexplainable again, and especially not for strangers. Siry and Jake and even Seltzer were one thing; hick cops or state troopers were quite another.

Speaking of explanations, where was that little twerp?

Well, he wasn't little, not actually. But he was twerp-like, for sure. What the hell was his story?

There was yet another mystery to put with all the others. The Witchblade had been strangely silent throughout all this. She had felt a dull throb or two, but that was all. As if the Blade had seen it all before and was not impressed. Even when the Werewolf was almost on her, it fairly yawned, as if it knew the Werewolf had no intention of attacking it, knew the creature had been charged with a more pressing assignment and was not about to bother with an adversary it could not best.

A flicker of a shadow. She turned, and there on the deck stood the twerp, looking in. He smiled sheepishly as he slid the door aside and stepped in.

"This your handiwork?" she asked him.

The kid inched closer, mesmerized by the sight of the mangled body, the blood. He seemed ambiguous about his feelings. Something like shock and a morbid glee vied for registration on his face. "No, man. Jesus, all that blood."

"The human body has quite a lot. You should have seen Anton and Sergei's apartment."

"Oh, man. Oh, man. That's really disgusting," the kid said, not able to shift his eyes away. "Almost took his head right off."

"Was this any of your doing?" she asked.

He shook his head. "No, no. I didn't do it."

"But did you conjure something that did?"

He looked at her. "Are you serious?"

"I'm totally serious. You do magic, don't you?"

"I dabble. It's long been an interest."

"But you can do real magic."

"I can do some things. But stuff like *that*? I can't do that."

She tried to gauge his sincerity. As far as she could tell, he was truthful. "Well, something did it. And that something wasn't normal. It was paranormal."

He asked, "What was it?"

"You didn't see it?"

"No. I heard some kind of animal noises. But I didn't see anything. Was it some kind of bear or something?"

"Bear? Hardly. It looked to me . . ." Sara scratched her head. It sounded so goofy. "You think you might possibly have conjured a werewolf?"

"Jesus Christ! Nothing I've been doing would conjure a freaking werewolf. Where did that crap come from? You sayin' a werewolf did this?"

"Same one I tangled with in the Russians' apartment, I think."

"You tangled . . ." He stepped back a few paces. Brooding, he walked slowly toward the windows. "Jesus. I don't know what the hell is going on. I gotta think about all of this."

"What went on in the woods?" Sara asked.

"That I have no idea. Some kind of big fire. I took off out the window, and that big dude was chasing me. Then I heard some kind of explosion, and I could see the woods burning."

"The big dude burned, too," Sara told him.

"I know. I saw him layin' out there. He's dead, too."

"What could have done it?"

"Have no idea."

She looked at him levelly. "We need to talk."

"You're a cop, aren't you?"

"Yeah."

"I thought so. Look, these guys were making me do the stuff. Extortion. I had no choice."

"Stuff?"

"Computer scams. I did some stuff for them. They liked it, and wanted more. Lots more. They wouldn't leave me alone. No one seems to be able to leave me alone, ever."

"I have a suggestion," Sara said. "Let's get the hell out of here."

"I second the motion."

"By the way, what's your name? I like to know who my partners in crime are."

"Merlin Jones."

As they headed south, the snow turned to rain and the road became a wet mirror.

It was not long before they were back in the more affluent areas of Connecticut. Huge mansions rolled past, some of the highest-priced real estate in the country.

"You don't think the guy in the house will talk?" Jones asked.

"Don't know. He's spent his life not talking to the police. Runs in the family. He might tell about me, might not. If they think he did it, and start to squeeze, he might blab. But I can't see why they'd think he did it. They'd go for the bear theory. If there are any bears in Connecticut, which I somehow doubt."

"I think there are."

"Whatever. Of course, I don't know what they'll make of Vladimir. Spontaneous combustion? A dragon loose?"

Merlin looked sharply at her. Then his gaze drifted out the window.

"Does that mean something to you?" Sara asked.

He shrugged. "I play Mah Jongg occasionally."

"Mah Jongg?"

"Yeah. Dragons. Red, green, white. You can't see white dragons in snow."

"I know nothing about the game. Never played it."

"Yeah, well in the States it's usually played by ladies of the club, that sort. But in China it's a man's game. Fast and furious and for lots of money."

"They play it in Chinatown?"

"Sure."

"And do you have any Chinatown connections?"

"That's how I ran afoul of Kontra. I refused to work for him, and the Triad courted me. I let them. All Kontra wanted to run were scams that the cyberpolice have been onto for years. He was going to get me busted, for sure. All he was about was money. He didn't appreciate the finer points. He didn't see it as the art it is."

"Hacking?"

"Yeah, hacking. He didn't appreciate the man-machine interface, you know? The cybernetic future dream. He didn't appreciate anything. And he didn't want to pay me what I was worth."

"It wasn't like the novels, was it?"

"Not really. It's just stealing. I know that. But . . . these guys, they just want to take."

"That's what they're into, Merlin. You didn't realize that?"

"I copped to it pretty early. I don't really need them, except . . . well, I had trouble paying the rent on time. I mean, in New York City, they bust your bank account for a pad the size of a closet. Kontra got me this big apartment, he made it easy. But he didn't pay me anything. Or anything substantial."

"You say you don't need them. Why don't you just rake in millions on your own?"

"It's not that easy. Most hackers aren't rich. Quite the opposite. We don't need that much money, really. But to make big money you need connections. You need money laundering. You need guys in Europe and Malaysia, overseas banks, all that stuff. Kontra had guys who could take the stuff I gave them and turn it into lots of cash. But the Triad will pay me what I'm worth."

"I don't know, Merlin. Seems to me some company could pay you one hell of a good salary for your skills. Ever consider going legit?"

"I do some work for legitimate companies, on a consultant basis. Sometimes."

"Like for who?"

"Irons International. I've done some work for Mr. Irons himself."

Sara was silent for a mile or two.

"Let's see if we can sum it up," she finally said. "Werewolves, dragons, Gypsy women . . ."

"Huh?"

"Kontra's grandmother."

"Oh, God, her. Like something out of a cult movie."

"Romanians, Russians. Werewolves. Dragons. Put it all together . . . wait. And another thing."

She fell silent again. The rain-slick road rolled by as Merlin regarded her.

"Yeah?"

"Know anything about a big bird?"

Merlin chuckled. "Right. *The Horror That Came to Sesame Street.*"

"Big bird in the sky. Coming out of a computer."

"Weird. What's *that* shit about?"

"You tell me. You're the magician."

"I do Kabbala. I mean, I study Kabbala. Numerology, mystical stuff. I do mandalas in Photo Shop. There's some really neat stuff . . ."

"I've heard of it. I mean, Kabbalistic magic. Know practically nothing about it. And mandalas . . ."

"From Sanskrit mysticism. I like to mix different ancient hermetic traditions. That's the kind of stuff I'm interested in. Ancient magic rituals, gods, spirits, demiurges. Fascinating stuff. I've been into it for years."

"Ever run into bird spirits?"

"Oh, of course. Many bird images in the ancient lore. The ibis-headed god of Egypt. That sort of thing."

"So what does it all mean? And what does Irons have to do with it?"

"He's interested in magic. Ancient lore."

"Oh, yeah," Sara said, nodding.

"You know him?" Merlin wanted to know.

Sara nodded. "I do."

"Then you know he appreciates the finer things. He appreciates me."

"That's nice. You like the finer things. Like what, for instance?"

"Art. I do art. Computer art, now. I started in oils long time ago. Studied it in school. But the computer's the greatest artist's brush to come along in years. Hasn't caught on in the academy yet."

"You're an artist?" Sara said. "Techno-nerd and artist. Not a common combo."

"Watch that 'nerd' stuff. I'm no nerd. I'm an artist of the Two Cultures that C. P. Snow talked about. Science and Art. Double-threat guy. That's me. I have things in mind, projects. Things never dreamed before. Works of art that . . . you have no idea."

"I'd be interested in hearing about them. Were you afraid that Kontra would kill you?"

"He knew he needed me. That was my hold over him. There are lots of hackers, but none of 'em can do what I do. I'm good, if I do say so myself."

"Just what kind of stuff were you doing in the magical area? Spells?"

"My stuff is New Age. It's modern, hip. No potions, no gypsy voodoo. It's just good luck-bad luck stuff. You increase your numerological odds, you stack the metaphysical deck in your favor."

"What's the bad luck part?"

"That's a weapon, sort of."

"Weapon?"

"Yeah. For your enemies. It's basic magic. You stack the deck in your favor and against your enemies' best interests. The effects can range from mild to lethal."

"Lethal?"

"Yeah, but I never do that. That involves invoking dark forces. I never do that. I just put a . . . well, you could call it a curse. You could call it bad karma. Or non-optimal feng shui."

"A curse isn't so modern," Sara said. "And who's say you didn't inadvertently invoke something you ought not to have invoked?"

"That's where the computer comes in. Precision. It's the modern magician's tool. I've pioneered this stuff. It's my technology. I'm the George Washington Carver of computer magic."

"So you put curses on people who get in your way."

"*Who mean to do me harm*," Jones said hotly. "Are you kidding? Of course I do. No law against it."

"Nope. No law. Except the moral one."

" 'Do what thou wilt shall be the whole of the law.' "

"Who said that?" Sara asked.

"Alistair Crowley."

"*He* was a wholesome guy," she muttered sarcastically.

"He penetrated to the mystical heart of the noumena."

"And he was great in the sack?"

Merlin grinned. "Matter of fact, he was reputed to be."

"Merlin, you have to face something. Whatever you've been doing, it may have led to what happened back there. And maybe what happened to Anton and Sergei."

"Can't be."

"Yes."

"No," Merlin insisted. "Take that dragon. Dragons are good luck signs in Chinese lore. That was a white dragon, the luckiest because they can't be seen to be hunted. At least in winter."

Sara nodded. "They don't kill people?"

"Not saying that. But dragons aren't evil in Chinese culture. Not like in the West."

"Okay."

Merlin gave an expansive shrug.

"Whatever that's worth."

She let him off on Seventh Avenue, around Seventh Avenue and West 34th Street.

"I guess you're not arresting me," Merlin said, holding the door open.

"I guess not. Nothing to arrest you for. Nothing anyone

would believe. As for the computer mischief, I'll leave you to the feds."

"Right. Well, take it easy."

"You, too. Don't let any non-optimal feng shui spoil your day."

"Yeah, don't take any wooden werewolves."

She thought about nothing much on her way to the station. After handing in the car at the motor pool, she walked to the squad room wanting nothing more than a cup of coffee. She had an hour to kill before starting her watch, and she wanted simply to relax.

"Pezzini."

She turned. "Hi, Jake."

Jake looked grim. "Sara, uh, this is hard."

"What is it?" She studied his face. "Something wrong?"

"Uh . . ."

She poured a cup of coffee and looked around for artificial sweetener. None here. All out. She made a mental note to order some. She turned and took notice that Jake wouldn't get out of her way. "Jake, what the hell is it?"

"Sara, the District Attorney wants to see you."

CHAPTER

SIXTEEN

Racketeering?" Sara practically shouted. "Are you insane?"

The newly-appointed interim District Attorney looked embarrassed. After all, he hadn't cooked this up. His deputies had.

One of them, Morrison, sat to the right of his boss's big desk. He was thin-faced and balding. "That's right. We may be able to proceed against you under the Racketeering Influenced and Corrupt Organizations Act. RICO. And we have at least five possible counts, possibly six, though the death of Charles Bromley is still officially an accident. We believe . . . that is, we have reason to believe that you are a hired assassin for the mob. A hit man. Uh, woman."

"Any particular mob?" Sara said. She was calm now, and resolved not to raise her voice again. The craziness of the charge had blindsided her.

"You are a known associate," Morrison went on, "of Lazlo Kontra . . . uh, the late Lazlo Kontra . . . who headed up a crime family out of south Brooklyn. You have been possibly linked to several murders that could have been mob executions. You were seen at one of Kontra's hideouts up in Connecticut. The State of Connecticut authorities want to talk to you about two deaths. We suspect your activities are interstate and possibly international."

"Crazier and crazier," Sara said.

"Detective Pezzini," said the District Attorney in a tone kindlier than his subordinate's, "don't you really think you should have counsel present?"

"I haven't heard anything yet to justify my retaining an attorney. I haven't heard you say you have any proof that I'm a hired assassin."

"The RICO law allows the prosecutor a lot of latitude," Morrison informed her. "It doesn't involve the usual 'beyond reasonable doubt' criterion. It's more like a civil case. Preponderance of evidence."

"Even if the evidence is as flimsy as what you have?" Sara asked pointedly. "Besides, RICO is a federal charge."

"We could easily refer the case to federal authorities."

"Why don't you?" Sara said.

Morrison started to say, "We will—"

The District Attorney cut him off. "It's a local matter for now. In fact, it's still really only an internal matter of the police department. Actually, we are really acting on information mainly supplied to us by Mr. Seltzer here."

Seltzer was sitting well back and away. But he was definitely present, as if auditing a course. "Yes, that's quite true. We've been watching Ms. Pezzini for a while. We've tracked her movements. For instance, she was observed heading for the Connecticut state line."

"But your operatives broke off surveillance," Sara said.

Seltzer's perpetual grin faded. "Internal Affairs has no authorization to cross state lines. We don't have jurisdiction.

But that didn't stop you." This last caused his lips to turn up at the corners again.

"Who says I crossed the line?"

"It's reasonable to assume . . ."

"Can you say honestly that they observed me crossing into Connecticut? That going to be your operatives' testimony?"

Seltzer didn't answer.

"I didn't think so."

"You were seen in Connecticut," Seltzer said.

"By whom?"

"By a known associate, albeit a so-called non-combatant, of a known crime syndicate boss. On the property of said boss."

"You going to rely on this witness's testimony?" Sara asked the DA.

"Uh . . . well, could he . . ."

"A witness who's spent his lifetime lying for this crime boss?"

"Two men ended up dead," Morrison said, "under very mysterious circumstances."

"Very interesting," Sara said. "But you have no reliable evidence. At least I've heard none so far."

"Your footprints were found in the snow by the state police."

"Snow?" Sara looked over at Seltzer innocently. "I didn't know it had snowed. Where?"

"Up in Connecticut."

"And you have these footprints?"

"Uh . . . the snow melted."

"Ohhhh," Sara said, as if a great epiphany had dawned.

Seltzer bristled. "Your footprints were found all over that apartment over the bar! In blood!"

"I was investigating a crime scene. I discovered the crime scene. Ask the bartender."

"Your supposed bartender never saw you, never heard of you. Can't identify you. And that other bartender you reported doesn't exist. No one's ever seen him."

"I don't make up bartenders, Mr. Seltzer."

"There must have two dozen people in that bar. We couldn't find one who'd corroborate your story."

"It's a mob night spot, owned and operated," Sara said.

Seltzer made a face. "The barbarity of that crime. The utter brutality! Those men were literally torn apart limb from limb."

"And I did it?"

"We haven't really said . . ." the DA tried to interpose.

"We don't know all the details," Morrison said.

"Any theories as to how I did it? Two big strapping guys?"

"There have been similar incidents in your past," Seltzer said. "Deaths of crime figures. I have your complete file. It makes for exciting reading. Sort of like a pulp novel."

"Who do you think I am? The Shadow? The Scarlet Pimpernel?"

"I think you're a mercenary," Seltzer said, "hiring yourself out to the highest bidder. I think you may be one of the best contract killers in the business."

Sara groaned and rolled her eyes. "I whacked Ashkenazie for Kontra. Then I whacked Kontra's gunsels. Then I whack Kontra along with another gunsel. Makes sense."

"As the Deputy District Attorney said, we don't know all the details, yet. But we will."

"I think she's a rogue cop," Morrison said. "A vigilante cop. Pulp novel? Oh, it's an old story. Organized crime figures are notoriously hard to nail. The temptation to do it extra-legally is just too much for some cops. Especially for a woman whose father was gunned down in a mob hit."

"I wonder what the judge will feel about introducing that kind of prejudicial evidence," Sara said. "They don't even let you bring up prior convictions, let alone prior victimizations."

Maybe it was the use of a variant of the word 'victim' that made Morrison look suddenly uneasy.

"Is he your best trial man?" Sara asked the DA in a chummy tone.

"Actually, Phil only does—"

"That's beside the point," Morrison quickly said. "We have more than enough for a prima facie case for . . ."

Here the DA's gimlet stare cut the ground out from under him.

". . . further investigation," Morrison finished.

Seltzer sat back and crossed his legs, looking disgusted.

"Now, that's exactly what I was thinking," the DA said magnanimously. "This is only a discussion, and we have to investigate this matter a little further. Detective Pezzini, we only wanted to let you know that some questions have been raised and they're serious questions, questions about professional conduct, and . . . and, uh . . . departmental procedure . . ."

The door opened and Joe Siry walked in.

"Albert!" he said with a huge grin. "Sorry I'm late."

"Joe!" The DA rose from his chair and came around the desk. He almost knocked Morrison over. "Joe, damn it, it's good to see you! How long has it been?"

"Too long. How's Edna? Is Tiffany in college yet?"

"Graduate school," Albert said, beaming.

"No! I'll be damned. Has it been that many years?"

"More years than I'll admit to."

"Listen," said Siry, "congratulations on the appointment. It must be hell stepping into someone's shoes. I mean, your predecessor suddenly taking ill like that."

"It hasn't been easy, Joe. It hasn't been easy."

"Albert, I want to talk to you about my girl, here. Pezzini. She's a fine officer, Albert. One of my best. Now, she's a little what you call unorthodox. You know how these kids are today . . ."

Seltzer and Morrison looked at each other, and in unison heaved a silent internal groan.

The room hummed. It was a quiet sound, a soft electronic purr. The room was underground, and the location was secret.

Mr. Irons's car had picked Merlin up. Merlin had been blindfolded, as usual.

He sat typing at a console that looked no different from a dozen similar in the room. Only the technician was extraordinary. He knew exactly what he was doing.

The Macro-Economic Modeling and Simulation Array sat behind him, occupying the central space of the polyhedral room. MEMSA was a thing of polyhedrons itself, composed of wedding-cake tiers surmounted by a topmost hexagon. A few tiny lights shone on its surface here and there. It was a real, as opposed to a movie, supercomputer. No patterns of dancing lights, no odd screens showing flashy nonsense. Its color was black, and it loomed darkly efficient over its various workstations. It seemed demanding, unforgiving. Mercilessly precise.

Merlin typed away. He understood the machine as did

no other technician in the facility. Machines had individual personalities, he believed, just like people. You had to get to know a machine. It had to get to know you. That went double for this particular machine and its highly sophisticated architecture. It bestrode the demarcation between smart machine and true Artificial Intelligence. No one really knew where it stood exactly with respect to that line.

It was of Japanese make, something so new that few engineers in the States had had a chance to take a look at it. Applications for the machine were largely nonexistent. It was in fact so new and so sophisticated that funds for the project that had produced it had gone dry, victim of recent Japanese economic doldrums. The programming for it had been relatively basic until Merlin had been given a chance to work with it.

He was proud of his accomplishments. The screen was showing some very interesting stock data from European exchanges, of great potential interest to day traders, data that shouldn't be available in real time. Or at all, really; not according to law.

The entrance door slid open and Kenneth Irons walked into the room. There was a look of quiet satisfaction on his face. On his way over, he passed his left hand lovingly over a smooth surface or two. "Merlin. Good evening."

"Mr. Irons. You should see this."

Irons came up to the workstation and bent over slightly. "Interesting. Wherever did you get that Ultra-High Level day trading screen?"

Merlin shrugged. "Cracked it, brought it in."

Irons chuckled. "Excellent. But we're not going into the day trading business, are we? I assume you're just flexing your muscles."

Merlin hit some keys, and the esoteric stock-trading tool disappeared. "Yeah, that's all."

Irons straightened up. "Playing the market is fine and there's money to be made. But we're going to make money the old-fashioned way. We're going to take it."

Merlin's turn to chuckle.

Irons stood and took in MEMSA. "Now, the machine's modality is still purely passive at this point?"

"It's still lurking. No one knows it's here. No one will ever know."

"No way for anyone to access, I take it?"

"No chance. No way to log on."

"It's complete isolated, yet infinitely sensitive to all the data conduits to which it is connected. Right?"

"It's a big sponge, soaking up the world's economic data."

"And once we perfect its active functions, this great bird will be able to dip its beak into every single transaction in the economic universe."

Merlin laughed openly. "You have a way of slinging the . . . inflated rhetoric."

Irons turned his head slightly. He was not irked. He smiled. "I admit it. I'm excited by this project. There's only one other lifetime ambition that could get my endorphins flowing this freely."

Merlin said, "I don't know about every single transaction. The main ones, sure. We'll be slicing baloney so fine . . . well, hell, Mr. Irons. There wouldn't be more than a penny missing in any one account after a trillion transactions. That's cutting it *thin*."

"Splendid. Very, very good. I'll be able to drop all the middle-men, such as your former employer, Mr. Kontra."

"But for the moment you'll still be dealing with the Organizatiya, along with all the other wiseguy groups?"

"I'm negotiating with Kontra's successor now," Irons said. "No problems. He's being very cooperative."

"You be the man, Mr. Irons, after we go on-line with this baby."

"When, Merlin? Can you give me a timetable when MEMSA can go completely operational?"

"Oh, give me a few months more to sandpaper some stuff, get out some of the bugs. You know this is a thorough-bred computer. I love the way it interfaces easily with just about every platform known to man and Gates. Speaks every language, knows every protocol, and what it doesn't know, it *learns*."

Walking around the big thing, Irons continued admiring it. "You think it's sentient."

"I think it's learning. It's a baby. Well, a kid. An adolescent."

"Interesting. I wonder . . . isn't there something called a Turing Test? Some rubric by which to ascertain true intelligence?"

"Yeah, theoretical as hell. I don't believe anything definite would come by such a test. You gauge intelligence as you would judge a work of art. I think intelligence is art, and vice versa."

"Interesting notion. Off the subject . . ."

Merlin looked up. "Yes, sir?"

"You mentioned meeting Sara Pezzini. The detective."

"Oh, was that her name? I don't think she told me."

"From your description, there's no one else it could have been. That was an extremely captivating story. From it we can assume that something paranormal has entered the picture."

"Definitely."

"Do you have any idea how it could have been introduced?"

"I'm not sure, sir. I dabble in magic myself, but I don't do dangerous stuff."

"You don't strike me as the dangerous type. Nevertheless, your former boss is dead of something that crossed the barrier between the mundane and the phantasmagoric."

"It wasn't me. I just put a mild curse on him. And his goons. They roughed me up one too many times. They think you can force a mind to think."

"They're thugs," Irons said. "And thugs run true to form. You were right to leave them without notice. They treated you abominably, judging by your reports."

"I appreciate your treatment of me, Mr. Irons. I'll be forever grateful."

"It's nothing. But let's get back to this paranormal element. What sorts of magic do you dabble in?"

"I'm about as eclectic as you can get. I have a CD of 5000 books on magic, the occult, mysticism, and hermetic tradition. It's a lot of stuff. I'm a student, really, not an adept. At least not yet."

"We're all still learning," said Irons. "But you say you put a 'mild curse' on Kontra. On his henchmen as well?"

"Well, yes, the ones who beat me up. But it wasn't black magic. It wasn't a death sentence. I messed with their karma. Their energy patterns, their material world lines."

"Well, it's still all very strange, what you told me. The B-movie aspects, the improbability of it all. I'll have to give it a great deal of thought."

"What does this detective have to do with anything?"

Merlin said. When Irons's hesitation became apparent, he added, "If you don't mind my asking."

"A complicated subject. Actually, her involvement piques my interest more than does the monster rally. All in the fullness of time, Merlin. All in the fullness of time."

Merlin went back to typing.

The big machine hummed quietly as Irons walked out.

"Now where did I put those directories?" Merlin said to the empty room as the door slid shut. He kept hitting keys, becoming increasingly frustrated.

"Hey," he suddenly said. "Where the hell did *that* come from? How did it get—?" He leaned back and gave the situation some thought.

Presently, he said, "Uh-oh."

CHAPTER
SEVENTEEN

The library's catalogue computer was simple to operate, but that also meant it was next to useless. Sara had put in MAGIC as the subject key word, and the machine had spewed out hundreds of titles. Better to narrow the search. What had Merlin talked about? Kabbala? Spelled with a K or a Q? The latter yielded little, so she tried K, and got about two dozen titles. The public library system had a lot of books.

She checked back to the call desk and found two titles she had previously requested. She picked them up, found an empty table, and sat down to read.

She read the introduction to one book. It made no sense whatsoever. She looked at the diagrams displayed. Groupings of little circles enclosing Hebrew script, all interconnected by lines. Clear as mud. She flipped through the other book. No help there. She read through a few pages of text and tried to divine the meaning. She was not sure there was any meaning to divine.

No, no. This stuff was extremely interesting and imaginative, but was of no use to anyone interested in the merely rational. Her situation was curiously ironic. There she was, sitting around with a magic talisman (for lack of a better term) on her wrist, and she couldn't make head or tail of any of this magic stuff.

She tried other books purporting to treat of the subject of the occult. They were all of a piece. They seemed to assume the reader understood the terms used in the text; however, there were few if any definitions or explanations of what the terms could mean, and those few offered tended to be conveniently obscure.

The historical books were interesting. She read through sections on magic in ancient Egypt, Mesopotamia, Persia, Israel, Greece, and Rome. She surveyed books on Gnosticism, alchemy, and divination. After going though the Arab philosophers and other medieval figures such as Albertus Magnus and Roger Bacon, she leafed through tomes on witchcraft and black magic. Also interesting were Nostradamus, Paracelsus, and the Christian Kabbalists. But none of this yielded any understanding of what was going on in her life.

A flicker of green hit her eye and she jerked her head up quickly. The computer screen at a nearby table glowed strangely. She watched it for a moment. It did nothing, but she could swear that it had flashed a green pattern. A familiar one, at that.

She shifted her eyes back to a discussion of the Rosicrucians.

Another flash of pale lime green. She didn't like being flashed.

She moved to another table, but after reading for a while, she became aware that a laptop was sitting directly behind her at the next table. It was open and whoever it belonged to had left it unattended, not a good idea in this city of petty pilferers. The owner was naïve or just care-lessly absent-minded. Whatever the case, the damned thing was flashing green patterns at her, behind her back. At least she thought so. Maybe she was just getting para-noid. Yes, that was it. She was definitely getting paranoid.

She moved anyway.

By the time she had to go back to the catalogue com-puter, she had forgotten about it. She did another subject search on OCCULT, got mostly the same listings, and then tried PARANORMAL.

ESP, UFOs, Bigfoot, and the Loch Ness Monster. The strange thing was that most of the books seemed to assume, more or less as a starting point, some reality to the phenomena they presented. There existed a skeptical literature, but it was skimpy by comparison to the true believer corpus. She noticed that Atlantis figured into a lot of this stuff. She dumped out of the catalog and went on the Internet to get what was available on Atlantis, the lost continent.

Faces.

She hit the ESCAPE button repeatedly, but that action did not get rid of the faces, the bland, faceless faces she had seen that night her laptop had suffered a fit of the heebee-jeebies, faces that sat atop robed bodies, all standing in groups staring out from cyberspace at her. She wasn't paranoid; there was no doubt it was her they were staring at her with those vacant eyes, jaws slack and loose. Rounded, moonlike pale faces that did not move, did not register emotion. They had an artificial cast. Per-haps they were not faces, but masks.

"What do you want?" she asked of them, the beings on the screen. "What do you want of me?"

She slammed the mouse until she got a conventional

screen. Ye gods, could these creepy guys have their own web page? Why not? Everyone else in creation did.

Maybe she should get her own web page, so anyone interested could log on and ogle the pictures she'd put up. Nude, maybe. She could charge by the download.

Internal Affairs would love that. They'd get her for international soliciting.

She took off for the open stacks to search the shelves for more books. The stacks seemed to go on forever. From the main aisle, she could not see their end in the shadows. Row upon row, shelf after shelf of dusty hardbacks. More books than anyone could read in ten lifetimes, perhaps more. Sometimes she got the idea that not only was there more knowledge than any one person could absorb, but that no one really knew how much knowledge actually existed. Not only are we ignorant, we are ignorant of how ignorant we are.

Flicker.

First flashes, now flickers. Well, she'd heard of hot flashes. Now these were hot flickers.

Whoa, steady girl.

She forced herself to focus and analyze what she was experiencing. It was as if someone were switching between two TV monitors, each with a shot of the same thing but in two different locations. One, the stacks as she saw them now. The other, stacks in a library somewhere else, some eldritch and unheard-of depository where books were huge, dusty ancient tomes with intricately tooled leather covers.

Flicker. Flicker.

She walked on despite her uneasiness, watching somebody riffle the deck of reality. The alternate tableaux began to acquire some duration. The musty books flickered, disappeared, and flickered back. She reached to touch one. It disappeared, replaced by a conventional book. Again, a flickering. She reached once more and ran her hand over ... it was not leather but the skin of some infinitely soft, infinitely alien thing. She shuddered and rubbed her fingers.

Masks appeared in the shadowed aisles. Groups of masks. The faces, the mask/faces, staring vacantly. They moved like ghosts, drifting over the quartz floor slabs.

She was no longer in New York. She was in another city, and this city's library had stacks as high as skyscrapers. They towered above, packed with artifacts all the way: scrolls, ledgers, tablets, steles, notebooks, parchments, stones, and boards, all bearing writing of some kind. And books, endless volumes in intricately crafted bindings.

She moved through the stacks, avoiding the advancing forms that confronted her. She turned corners and ran, stopped, cast a look behind. Ran again. She found an aisle and scurried down it, expecting hands to reach out from the shelves and drag her into their depths.

The flickering had stopped. She was in the alternate reality, and the reality of her experience was only an occasional flashback.

She saw an end to the stacks, an open area, and sprinted for it, and when she ran out into its vastness was shocked that the ceiling was lost in mists above. The place must have been seventy stories high, a vast atrium. Her footsteps echoed in droves, endless reverberations that bounced off lofty groined vaults and flying buttresses. She felt like an ant skittering through a medieval cathedral.

Sara Pezzini.

She did not know where the voice originated and did not want to look.

Sara Pezzini.

It was a voice that could not be human, its quality alien and remote and improbable. It could have been a synthesized voice; if so, was a synthesis of something that should not have existed in the first place. But there were human contours to it, and an underlying sense of something resembling emotion. The emotion was . . . urgency? Desperation?

Sara . . .

They knew her name, these specters, these eidolons, and she wished mightily that they did not. She didn't want them in possession of something so vital a part of her. Her name was something sacred. Their very knowledge of it was a violation of some kind.

She was overcome with a revulsion at these creatures, a gut-felt repugnance. She did not have a sense of evil so much as a sense of the complete absence of all that was human and natural. If any being could be unnatural, these creatures were.

Demons?

Why not? It was as good a word as any to describe them. But she thought it very strange that she got no impression of malevolence. Not like the Bird.

Screeeeeeeee . . .

Had she summoned the bird merely by thinking of it? She stopped and looked up. Something was flying in the place's upper reaches, lost in gray fog of distance, a dark something flapping and fluttering, a vague shape, a blur of motion, a click of talons, and what emanated from this was a longing to swoop, to snare, to clutch, to rend.

"Hi, there," Sara said to it.

Flicker.

She was running through the lobby of the public library. She skidded to a stop. A few people were looking at her. She felt like an idiot.

"You okay?" asked a tall black guy in passing.

She nodded. Sheepish and not wanting to be taken for a schizophrenic on the loose, she walked as calmly as she could through the revolving doors and out onto the street.

Sanity, always an issue with her. Perhaps the Witchblade was a huge bloc of symptoms, plain and simple, symptoms of a pathology that existed only in her mind.

Why, why had she been picked to bear the Witchblade? Maybe she could discover the reason if she knew what the Witchblade itself was all about. Down through the ages, it had chosen its champions, and they had all been women.

But perhaps that was all in her mind. Perhaps these transformations only existed in her perception, and everything that happened during them could be explained rationally. Maybe Kontra had been killed by a marauding bear instead of a werewolf.

Ah, but what was a marauding bear doing in a Brooklyn apartment? Explain that.

Nevertheless, doubts about her sanity recurred on occasion, and this was one. Even if the damned thing were real, it would drive anybody crazy.

Flicker.

"Damn it," she said, determined to keep walking no matter what.

Flicker flicker flicker flicker flicker flicker flicker . . .

That city again, the city of impossible buildings, the New York of alternate reality, a city of spires and perches, with doorways half a mile in the air, a metropolis of avian beings, a place that did not, could not exist, flickering in and out of existence, flickering like some old silent film grinding through a hand-cranked projector. She remembered her father taking her to Coney Island . . . in the old Penny Arcade there were still nickelodeons consisting of cards with a single frame of film printed on them. You cranked the machine and the cards came up one by one. The faster you cranked, the faster the action went and the faster the flickering became. This was as if someone had shuffled two stacks of cards with different scenes. A frame of one was followed by a frame of the other, and so on.

The shifting of realities took on the action of a stroboscope; the flickering speeded up and became almost blinding. She had to shield her eyes in order to walk. Even the pavement changed beneath her feet, from ordinary concrete to some shiny obsidian substance. But she walked, more determined than ever. She was going home, and that was all there was to it. Damn Greek choruses, damn strange birds, damn shifting realities. Damn all.

Yes, but where did she live in *this* city?

And where did that Greek temple come from, speaking of choruses?

Well, it looked something like a Greek temple. Sort of. It had columns, very high ones; it also had friezes, bas-reliefs, and all the rest of the architecture, all distorted somehow, bent through a geometry that was not even non-Euclidean. It was just damned weird.

She walked across a street of paving stones like black mirrors and mounted the steps in front, steps that went up at least two stories. She climbed steadily until her legs began to ache, but kept climbing, her footsteps echoing.

At least she reached the floor of the temple and walked

through a forest of columns before coming under the distant roof. The columns, long, fluted, and slightly oval, continued for a stretch, then gave onto an open area. She stopped and took in the huge statue standing in the central area.

It was a statue of herself in full Witchblade regalia.

She stared at it for an interminable period, not comprehending, not able to process the data her eyes were feeding her. Gradually she became aware that she was not alone in the temple.

The Chorus stood arrayed at the foot of the statue. Slowly they all turned to face her, and she regarded them questioningly.

"What do you want?"

To worship you . . .

It was an answer she did not want to hear. She looked up at her own image. The statue was of heroic proportions, a massive figure of silver and gold with glints of other precious substances, perhaps but not limited to onyx, amethyst, and amber. The statue had wings sprouting from a riot of swirls and other metallic flourishes. Jewels sparkled everywhere. The base was inlaid with semiprecious stone in eye-catching arabesques. There was an alien nature to the thing, imparted not by the subject of the work but by the artist. This was not the work of a human artist; this was the work of a being not human at all.

"I'm flattered," she said to the Chorus. "But no, thanks."

She turned and walked out of the temple. No one tried to stop her.

She did not have to descend the two-story stairway. Once out from under the roof of the temple, New York flickered back into existence, and she was on the side-walk.

She knew where she had to go and it was a long walk, so she hailed the first cab that came by.

Maybe her luck was changing, she thought. The damned cab actually stopped.

CHAPTER

EIGHTEEN

Sophia pushed buttons on the telephone while Baba sat by the window, looking out. Sophia looked back at her.

"It's the only thing we can do. The only justice."

Baba didn't move her eyes from the setting sun. "How much will it cost?"

"A lot of money. Can you think of money now? He was your grandson."

"You never cared for him. Only his money, his position, his power."

"I loved him. He was my husband."

"He had other women."

"That means he wasn't my husband?"

"So," said Baba, "you will take up his business."

"Why not? A woman can't run a business?"

"It's man's work, this business."

"You're old-fashioned," Sophia told her. "Mind your own business."

"I do, I do. Everyone thinks I want to meddle. I don't."

"Then shut up. Hello? Mr. Strauss? Oh, I wish to speak to him. Yes. Yes. Very well. Please tell him that an old friend, Sophia Kontra, wishes to speak with him. I'm calling long distance. Yes, an old friend. He knew my husband." Sophia turned again. "They're getting him."

"How much are you paying the telephone company for this call?"

"Who knows?" Sophia said testily. "Who cares?" She waited patiently. Then: "Hello? Mr. Strauss? This is Sophie. Yes, it is. How nice to hear your voice. Thank you, thank you . . ."

"It's not a good thing, this," Baba said. "It's an evil thing we do."

Sophia went on talking.

The view from a Central Park West apartment is spectacular. The park spreads out like your own personal enchanted forest, and from penthouse height the derelicts, addicts, and gangbangers could be munchkins for all you are concerned.

At night, the park seems the dark domain of dragons and demons. Living in New York is made easier by a rich imagination. It also helps if you're just plain rich.

Kenneth Irons walked away from the window. For all that his imagination—as well as his stock portfolio—was one of the richest on earth, his mind was not on enchanted forests this night. His man had announced a visitor, one he knew well. He was ready to receive her any time of the day or night. He had directed his man to admit her forthwith and send her up.

He sat down in a chair in the picture gallery and waited among oil paintings of heroic women, former wielders of the Witchblade. Amongst his favorites was a portrait of Jeanne d'Arc. Joan astride a horse in full battle regalia. The best known of all the sentient gauntlet's bearers and wearers.

The tall door to the study opened and Sara Pezzini stepped in. She was dressed, as usual, in what he regarded as rags. But on her even rags looked good. Her jeans were usually particularly tight and the T-shirt under her jacket was always undersize, allowing her feminine lineaments to come through nicely. She was tall, thin, well-proportioned, and had a face that could launch several navies. Legs up to the neck. Oh, those legs. And there were other parts of her that shaped up just as well.

He sometimes permitted himself the luxury of simple lust.

"Sara," he said warmly.

"Hello, Ken. What have you been up to?"

"I'm always up to something. How has it been with you?"

"Up to my butt in alligators, as usual."

"I envy those alligators," Irons said with a grin. "Do sit down."

Sara took a seat on a luxurious chaise. "My question wasn't an idle one. Have you been up to anything supernatural lately?"

Irons looked surprised. "Why, what a question. What would bring you to ask it?"

"Strange things have been happening around the Witchblade lately."

Irons had avoided looking at the bracelet since she had come into the room. Now he slowly shifted his eyes and took it in. It was in its quiescent state, taking the form of a simple bracelet. He had seen it in many configurations since he had unearthed the artifact in Egypt years ago.

"What sorts of strange things?" Irons asked.

"Apparitions that do murder in fairly grisly ways. And another phenomenon. The intrusion of a very weird world on ours. This involves a few more apparitions."

"What sort of world?"

"Like nothing I've seen before. I haven't had a lot of time to think it through, but it may have something to do with the apparitions, and it might not."

"That's . . . helpful."

"Okay, it's not. They've got to be related, though."

"All right. What forms do these apparitions take?"

"At least three kinds. One is for all intents and purposes a werewolf, or something like it. Another is a dragon. Another, related to the strange world thing, is a bird of some kind, and associated with it are humanoid forms."

"Werewolf," Irons mused. "Interesting."

"Know anything that can connect up with that?"

"What's the Witchblade's interest been?"

"It's interested," Sara said. "But it's not telling me what it thinks."

"It wouldn't," Irons said. "It's always been rather closed-mouthed."

Sara laughed. "I guess you could put it that way."

"I was being ironic. Let me think."

"I have a connection. Lazlo Kontra was taken out by the werewolf. Lazlo Kontra was Romanian by birth. He has a Romanian grandmother who walked out of a Lon Chaney, Jr. picture."

Irons brooded a moment. "So that's why my sources were so confused on the method."

"I'll bet it didn't sound like a mob hit."

"No. Jobs of that kind are usually done with minimum

mess, except on occasion. So Kontra was done in by this supernatural factor, whatever it is."

"No doubt," Sara said. "And I don't have any ready explanation for it. Except for a crazy one."

"What's that?"

"A crazy nerd kid. Computer hacker. Brilliant kid, but a little odd. Messes with magic. But how he could be summoning monsters . . . what's wrong, Ken?"

Irons had grown a subdued expression of concern. By the time Sara had spoken, it was gone.

"You know this kid," Sara said.

"You really took me by surprise," Irons said. "I shouldn't be surprised by this time. You have a way about you."

"Don't try to snow me, Irons. The kid's name is Merlin. Know him?"

"You've already guessed it. He's been doing some work for me. Consulting."

"On what?"

"That's my business, Sara. Let's say it's a special project."

"Anything to do with magic?"

"Not in the least. But now you tell me Merlin is living up to his name."

"He admitted to a possible motive. He told me without a thought that he could be admitting to a murder. He claimed he didn't intend for his victims to die."

"Interesting, interesting," Irons said, rather too abstractedly.

"I think you know the motive, too. I think you might have hired him away from Kontra."

"I considered Merlin a free lance. Didn't really give it a thought. Actually, he's been working for me for a while."

"I see," Sara said, sitting back.

"If I gave him a motive . . ."

"I don't think you did. I think it was between Kontra and Merlin, and magic was used to settle the dispute, however inadvertent the outcome was."

"Glad to hear you don't suspect me of contributing to this grisly business."

"I've known you long enough to suspect that you had a hand in somewhere."

Irons tried to look pained. "I'm hurt."

"I also know that this whole business has something to do with computers."

This also hit Irons from an unexpected direction. "Indeed," was all he would allow.

"Yeah. Funny thing, the bird and the humanoid creatures came at me from out of my laptop."

"They came at you?"

"Reaching for me, and I think reaching for the Witchblade. Odd. It wasn't particularly threatening, that time. On other occasions, the bird was a little different. It seems to have a grudge against me."

"Curiouser and curiouser," Irons commented. "How about the other creatures? The werewolf, for instance."

"I beat it up pretty good."

"Congratulations."

"The dragon didn't give me any trouble at all. But it killed Kontra's gunsel. Burnt him to a crisp."

"Ah, as dragons are wont to do, no doubt. All very, very interesting."

Sara let out a breath. "Yeah. Like a massive traffic accident."

"Right. You have to look, don't you?" Irons said.

"Any ideas, Ken?"

"A few. I'll let you know if any of them become coherent. They aren't right at the moment."

"Neither are mine. I can't understand the bird thing. It seems unrelated. Whereas the werewolf and the dragons are definitely something some goofy kid would dream up. Or pick up from his environment."

"His environment?"

"He was working for a Romanian. I mentioned the guy's grandma. That also explain the Vlad connection . . ."

"Eh?"

"Another thing entirely. It doesn't fit, not quite."

"You have a puzzle here with rather disparate pieces," Irons said.

"Sure do. And I think you do, too, Ken. Though you're not admitting anything."

"I don't know what to admit. I'm as confused as you."

She leaned forward and looked him straight in the eye. "You may be telling the truth. It's hard for me to tell, most of the time."

"Sara, that's a roundabout way of calling me a liar."

"Really," Sara said, getting up. She began a casual tour of the picture gallery. It was not her first, but the depictions of her predecessors were an endless source of fascination.

Irons got up and followed her. "You know, I still claim the Blade as mine."

"Never said it wasn't," Sara told him.

"Yet you'll be walking out of here with it. You could call that theft, in a way."

"You could. You won't. We both know why I have to wear it. You can't, and neither can anyone else. With the possible exception of Ian Nottingham. But he's a special case."

"True," Irons said gravely. "Undeniably true. So I suppose our little agreement will continue."

"Until we get to the bottom of the Witchblade's mystery. By the way, I saw him recently."

"Oh, you did?" Irons said brightly. "And how is old Nottingham?"

"Doing pretty good for a dead guy."

"He always was resourceful."

"That doesn't surprise you?"

"What, that he's keeping up appearances? Stout fellow, and all that."

"Maybe I saw his ghost," Sara said.

"Perhaps you did. I don't know, and really don't care to follow the careers of former employees. Once they go off the payroll, my interest in them ceases."

"Yes, once you threw him out the window, you pretty much didn't care where he landed."

"As the old song says, 'That's not my department, said Warner von Braun.'"

"Tom Lehrer," Sara said.

"You remember Tom Lehrer?" Iron said, mildly surprised. "You're not old enough."

"I have him on CD."

"You're a culturally literate heroine-goddess."

"That's exactly what the strange guys in the bird world think of me. They say they want to recruit me as their goddess."

"They speak to you?"

"In a sense. That particular statement was extremely clear."

"Extraordinary. You should be flattered. I was just thinking. Instead of headhunters, these people have godhunters?"

"I wonder if there's a signing bonus," Sara mused.

"Well, good luck in your new career."

"Not interested in the job. I have a job investigating homicides in the City of New York."

Irons said, "Do you think that in any universe you could conceive of, let alone the City of New York, you could connect me with the death of Lazlo Kontra, or anyone else?"

"Sure. I could get the DA to believe that one of your employees did it."

"By magic?"

"I don't have to bring magic into the picture. No one would believe it anyway. All I have to supply is a motive, and you start to look like the gray eminence behind all the killing that's been going on. Oh, your lawyers will protect you. You'll get off, but your reputation . . . ?"

"I see what you mean. Nasty stuff, Sara. Why?"

"Let's say I have a few scores to settle with you."

"I'm crushed that you think me an enemy."

"Ken, I think you're up to something. I don't know what it is, but I'd like to find out. I'm going to find out."

"I see."

"Good night, Mr. Irons."

"Good night, Sara. Do drop in anytime."

When she had gone and Irons had been left alone to contemplate, yet again, the pictures in his gallery, his manservant opened the door to tell him he had a phone call.

He walked to his desk. "Irons here."

"Erwin Strauss," came a familiar voice. "Forgive the late call."

"Yes, what is it?"

"I have been offered a very challenging contract. It's on the girl. Your girl."

"Interesting."

"I know your association with her. I have never quite understood the nature of it, but as you are the most powerful man in your city—you are, in a sense, the boss of bosses—I am notifying you of my intention to take the contract."

"I suppose you don't want to tell me who your clients are."

"They are amateurs who don't know what they are asking. They phoned me. Imagine that. Fortunately, I forestalled any mention of business and got in touch with them via a secure line."

"I suppose I can't change your mind," Irons said.

"With money? Yes. One billion dollars."

Irons laughed derisively. "In small bills, I suppose?"

"You will wire it to my account."

"That's rather steep," Irons said flatly.

"True. But the girl means quite a lot to you."

"I can't deny it. But a billion? Even if I would permit myself to be blackmailed . . ."

"You can't prevent it. I am doing it, Mr. Irons. One billion, or the girl dies, and that she is some kind of sorceress will not make a difference."

"Oh. And just how do you propose to take her down?"

"That is my business."

"Nevertheless . . ." Irons could only say.

"Very well. I have given you fair warning. Good bye."

Irons began, "Mr. Strauss, I think you fail to—"

But Strauss had hung up.

CHAPTER
NINETEEN

It's one of the bad ones," a patrolman said in passing to Jake and Sara as they entered the crime scene. "Bloody as hell."

"As if murder can be anything but," Jake commented to Sara as they walked into a spacious apartment on the upper West Side.

"Looks like murder by cable guy," another patrolman greeted them. He was standing in front of a wall that looked like a Jackson Pollock painting in blood. At the base of the wall lay a body with about as many bullets in it as a body could contain without being classified as an alloy of lead.

"What led to that conclusion, officer?" Sara asked.

"We have at least two people saw the cable truck double parked outside, saw the cable guy enter. Residents then heard lots of what they called 'popcorn popping.' A silenced Mac 10, we're thinking."

Jake said, "Are you bucking for a promotion, Patrolman . . . ?"

"Linaweaver. Matter of fact, I'm taking the sergeant exam next week."

"Very good work, all that deduction."

"Thank you, sir. Uh . . . actually, I'm just reporting the facts as we got them."

"So we have witnesses to the cable guy," Sara said, "to the shots, and what else?"

"Uh, I called up the cable company. The victim was scheduled to get a digital box installed today. Real cable guy is working on the other side of town. Ergo, this was obviously a fake cable guy."

"Aren't they always?" Jake said.

Sara asked, "No one saw the cable guy leaving?"

"No one's come forward. But the truck's gone."

"Okay," Sara said. "Thanks, Linaweaver."

"So we have a cable guy who's a homicidal maniac?" Jake said.

"No, we have an assassination with the hit man posing as a cable TV company employee."

"You think the victim's mobbed?"

"Sounds like a pro job," Sara said. "Who would suspect the cable guy of being a hit man?"

"No one. Right, you let him right in."

"Has all the earmarks of a hit."

Jake nodded toward the wall. "What do you think of those marks?"

"Don't make jokes."

"I'm not," Jake said. "I was about to make the comment that there have been some pretty spectacular hits lately. And this one looks like another."

"Linaweaver?" Sara called.

"Yes, sir. Ma'am?"

"Didn't you leave something out of your report?"

"Uh, I don't think so, ma'am."

"No?"

Linaweaver frowned and thought.

Sara prodded, "The name of the victim? Whose apartment is this?"

"Oh! Sorry, sorry. Uh, name's Bubnov." Linaweaver fished out his notepad and thumbed through it. "Ivan . . . uh . . . Ilyich Bubnov."

"Need I say more?" Jake asked.

"Right," Sara said, taking a stance a few feet from the wall. "Close range. Perp was standing about here. Opened up and emptied the magazine."

"Wonder why," Jake said. "Wanted to do a thorough job, or he liked to see the blood spatter?"

"Little of both?" Sara said. "Linaweaver, is the victim the tenant here?"

"Uh, yes. Super ID'd him. Sorry, I should have said that."

"Yes, you should have, right straight off. Hope they don't have that question on the sergeant's exam."

"Sorry."

Linaweaver slinked away.

"Well, another mob-related death."

Sara still stood looking at the wall. Jake watched her for a moment.

"Sara?"

She glanced at the bracelet on her wrist. Then she said, "No."

"No?"

"Right," Sara said.

"No, what?"

"It's not related. Not related at all. For all that spatter, looks like it could be hanging in the MOMA."

"Huh?"

"Never mind. Let's do our job and get all we can out of the place. But I can tell you now it's not going to connect up with anything."

Jake and Sara were the last ones out of the apartment. The paramedics, techs, uniformed officers, and all related personnel had cleared out a least a half-hour before the detective partners came out the front door of the building.

"So he was nominally in real estate, but head of an extortion ring," Jake commented as they walked down the avenue. "Nice things people are up to behind the façade of respectability. You ready for lunch?"

"Yeah, I'm starved," Sara said. "Façades are what it's all about. Your modern mobster wants a low profile. The lower the better. The smart ones do, anyway."

"Street gang types aren't among the smart ones, I guess."

"There's always plenty of that type. I'm talking about the upper echelons."

"Yeah, they always have a way of protecting themselves. Except sometimes they don't. Like our Comrade Bubnov. Oh wait, do they use 'comrade' as a title anymore? In Russia, what do they call—?"

The shot sounded like the explosion of a fairly good-sized firecracker. The sound came from high up, a roof or a window.

Jake's mouth was still open and in the middle of his last sentence. He closed it and hit the pavement behind a parked car. "Sara!"

She was still standing in the middle of the sidewalk, her right arm raised.

Covering his head, Jake peered between his fingers. He

saw something he had seen before. A strange gauntlet, a mailed glove of some kind, busy with swirls and arabesques of metal filigree, covered Sara's right hand and forearm.

Jake knew what had happened, but didn't want to believe it. Besides, he didn't have time to think about it just now.

Another shot came, and with it the whining ping of a ricochet. She had deflected another bullet off her gauntlet. Jake got to his knees and searched for the source of the fire.

"Jake, stay down!"

He obeyed. Another shot, and another, both whanging off the gauntlet. Sara's arm was a blur of motion.

How? How? Jake screamed in his mind.

Sara was looking up, searching the high vantage-points. She lifted her left arm. "There! Jake, I'm the target. Get across the street and cover the back of the place. This creep's not going to slip away if we can help it. Call backup now!"

"Right!" Jake yelled, getting up and dashing out from cover. He ran across the street as fast as he could make it. The building was a typical apartment for this neighborhood, a lobby locked to nonresidents, a security man sitting at a desk in the lobby. Jake had to pound on the door and wave his badge before the security-doorman would let him into the lobby, where he phoned for backup and a SWAT team to back up the backup.

Sara looked up and down the street. Jake did the same. Arrayed all around them were SWAT team members, regular police, and county cops. Around the corner lurked fireman, paramedics, news reporters, and the general public, all milling about. They had the building covered from all angles. Jake had gotten to the back door immediately after phoning in.

Sara was ticked at him for that. But he had felt bad about leaving Sara all alone out there. He'd run to the back fire doors as soon as he got off the phone. They had been closed, and opening them would have tripped alarms. He was fairly sure that no one could have left the building.

Sara turned around and sat on the concrete with her back against a squad car. "He's gone."

"How?" Jake asked. "Most of the residents are still in the building. Maybe he's hiding out in an apartment, holding the tenants hostage."

"We'll screen everybody inside. We won't find him. I just have a feeling."

"Could the shots have come from another place?"

"I saw the barrel. High-powered rifle, big scope, up on the roof."

"Okay, I believe you. On the roof."

"Of that building," Sara said.

"So he has to be still in there," Jake said without feeling.

"No, he does not."

"How'd he get out? And so quick?"

"I don't know. But obviously we are dealing with an accomplished pro."

"Know why he's out to get you? Because I think you're right, you were the target. He didn't even try a shot at me."

"I don't know why. I don't know who. But the rest is obvious."

"Obvious? Why do you say that?" Jake asked.

"This thing is telling me," Sara said with a glance at her bracelet.

Jake was again reminded that she seldom referred to the thing on her wrist, and when she did it was usually in an indirect manner. "Okay, but what is it that's obvious?"

"Let's call these guys off and go in and question the residents. We are going to hit every apartment. And I want to look into every apartment that doesn't have somebody answering the door."

"Sara, we're not papered for searches."

"I didn't say search. I said look into."

"Oh. I guess we can do that thing."

They did that thing, and after talking to just about everyone in the building, mostly aged Jewish people of foreign birth and/or recent citizenship, Sara realized that the search was hopeless.

"Still up for lunch?" Jake asked when everyone was readying to go back whence he had come.

The SWATs were packing equipment into cases, the police were gathering up barricades and yellow police tape. The paramedics had pulled up to the front of the building in case any resident had heart trouble caused by the commotion. The firemen, having better things to do, had left.

"You're incorrigible," Sara said.

"I'm human. I have to eat at least once a day."

"Listen, you go grab a dog or something, I'll run into that Starbucks across the street. We have an interview at one, remember?"

"Yeah, okay. Thought I saw a street dog vendor when we arrived. Wonder where he got to?"

"I'll meet you at the coffee shop," Sara said, heading for the intersection.

She wasn't dejected. Just frustrated. This was the most frustrating Witchblade snafu to date. Not only did it all make zero sense, it didn't even—

"Miss Pezzini."

"Huh?"

Sara whirled. Out of the proverbial dark alley stepped a man in a utility work uniform. He looked strange. Something about even the shape of his head was sinister. Every line in his forehead and face exuded menace. Yet overall there was something bland, almost bureaucratic about him. The prosaic malevolence of a genocidal civil servant, a true sense of the banality of evil, radiated from him like an aura.

Sara took an instinctive step backward.

"My name is Edwin Strauss. I have been hired to assassinate you. I intend to do just that."

He spoke with a pronounced middle-European accent, but with overtones of culture and refinement. Sara took another step back.

"This was a test, a test of your powers. You passed admirably. You did not even look to where the first shot came from before you blocked it. Truly remarkable, Miss Pezzini. To say that your powers are extraordinary would be an understatement by several factors of magnitude."

Sara said simply, "What do you want?'

"I always try to meet my subjects and introduce myself. It makes the interaction a more human one. I do it whenever possible—*whoops!*"

Sara had made a motion. Strauss had his gun out, as if by magic.

"Hand me your weapon please, and please step back from the street. We are conspicuous here. Come into the alley. I wish to speak with you."

Sara obeyed, handing him her revolver as she stepped by him. In the alley, she turned to face him.

"Your talisman is fast to defend you but not as quick on the offensive. Curious. I suppose I still have much to learn about it. But I am learning very quickly."

"How do you come to know about me?"

"I know many things I should not know. That is how I stay alive in this world, Miss Pezzini. I know about you, about Kenneth Irons, and perhaps a bit more."

"Perhaps," Sara said. "And then again, you could be lying."

"I don't lie," Strauss said.

"How did you get out of that building so quickly?" Sara asked pointedly.

"Ah. But I did not say I would divulge my trade secrets."

"Then say what you have to say. I was on my way to lunch."

"My apologies. But I have said it already. I have introduced myself, and have announced my intentions. That is sufficient."

"Who hired you?"

"Again, a secret that hired assassins guard with their lives. Sorry. I must decline to answer."

"Okay, you said your piece. Here's mine. You won't kill me, and I will catch you and put you away for a long, long time. There's lots to explain lately, and you are the likeliest explanation to come along yet. In fact, you're a welcome sight. You're going to come in mighty handy, mister."

"Oh, my." Strauss was grinning from ear to ear in a ghastly rictus that was not at all a pleasant sight. "You do have spunk. Oh, my. I think you may prove a great deal of fun."

"I'm so glad for you."

"I'm not alone, you know. There is a veritable team out for your demise."

"I hope you and your chums have all the fun you can get. You'll be having none in Sing Sing."

"Ah, Sing Sing! The very name rings with the sound of high crime and misdemeanor. An American institution in every sense of the word. I should be proud to be an inmate. But I must decline the offer. I have never come close to being apprehended. I do not intend to be caught now, or ever."

"Well, I guess it's rah rah, team, then."

"Indeed. However, it also must be admitted you will be a challenging subject. This test tells me that ordinary methods will not be sufficient. Next time, I might be one of a number of . . . shall we say, unnatural adversaries?"

"Got it."

"Yes. You see, I am not unacquainted with the occult. Neither are you, as evidenced by . . . that." Strauss gestured with his gun at the bracelet, which, while he had been talking, had slowly grown and metamorphosed into its gauntlet form, albeit a subdued and compact variation.

"Okay," Sara said simply.

Strauss looked at his gun. "Strange. Standing here like this, part of me is wondering why I couldn't just shoot you now and get it over with. But, as I see, you would simply ward off the bullet in magical fashion, the shot would draw attention, and I would be in a pickle."

"Very interesting," Sara said. "Here's something to think about. If that gun is doing you no good, what's preventing me from clouting you with this mitten I have on and hauling you in right now?"

"I told you I was not alone. I am for the moment protected from you by magical means. You see this?" Strauss reached into a pocket and pulled out a bright orange feather. The color was more than iridescent. It was almost incandescent. "It is a feather of the firebird."

"Eh?"

"The firebird. Its feathers are magical and can ward off any attack. I am thus protected from you. The gun is simply for psychological effect."

"Let's do an experiment," Sara said, stepping forward and reaching for him with the gauntlet hand.

He disappeared.

"You see? Behind you, Miss Pezzini."

She turned. He was indeed standing behind her. She lunged and tried again. Again, he vanished momentarily, only to reappear about twenty feet farther up the alley.

"Sorry," Strauss said. "We are at a stalemate. I can't hurt you, and you can't lay a glove on me. Now is not the time of our final confrontation. So I will simply say good-bye. Good-bye, Miss Pezzini, and good luck to you. I will leave your weapon in a trash receptacle in the back alley. Sorry for the inconvenience."

"Thanks," Sara said cheerily. Then her smile faded as she saw the lettering on the back of his work suit: MAN-HATTAN CABLE..

She watched him disappear into the shadows.

CHAPTER

TWENTY

When Sara and Jake reported back at the end of their watch, there was a note in Sara's message box. It was from Siry. It read simply: *Sara, see me immediately. Joe.*

She knocked on his door. For some reason the frosted glass panel struck her as quaint. It had never occurred to her before. She didn't know how old the precinct house was; doubtless it was ancient.

Speaking of which, Joe Siry was looking his age today. The lines of his face seemed deeper, darker, and his eyes had receded into their sockets. He looked as though he had done himself up in stage makeup to play an older part. Maybe it was just his somber expression.

"I take it the news isn't good," Sara said, standing at the door.

"You are in some deep do-do," Siry said in a sepulchral tone.

"That isn't good," she replied. "How not good is it?"

"You do a bad impression of Johnny Carson."

"I thought it was Ed McMahon. You're at least trying to crack a joke. That must mean I'm not being indicted."

"You're awfully close to being indicted. Well, let's just say that Morrison wants to convene a grand jury, but I still have Albert convinced you're a good cop who's simply misunderstood. A maverick, you go your own way, get into lots of trouble bucking authority, that sort of thing. He's bought it so far, and he's still buying it. But Morrison's been working on him, and just about has him worn down. Old school ties aren't unbreakable. They only hold up under so much weight. And your indictment is hanging by a thread."

"They still don't have any evidence I'm a hit girl for the mob."

"No, I don't think they do," Siry agreed. "What they have is a lot of gruesome crimes that have only one connecting factor: you. You are very handy and not very well liked in some quarters. Partly because you refuse to toe the line, partly because you're a girl. Uh, I'm sorry, woman."

"Funny, around you I always feel 'girl' is the more appropriate term," Sara said as she came in and took a seat.

Siry grunted. "I'll take that as a compliment. As I was saying, you are prime material for taking the fall."

"Oh, yeah? I play the sap for no one, see. Gosh, Cap. Let's do more 1930s B-movie dialogue. It's fun."

"Goddamn it!"

Sara sobered up and sat up. "What's wrong, Joe?"

"Here I go to bat for you, trying to save your skinny little ass, and you sit there and make silly jokes. Don't you think an indictment is going to reflect badly on me? Or do you always think just of yourself?"

"Sorry, Joe. I didn't mean to hurt you. I was just trying to cheer you up. You look tired. I've been worried."

"I look tired? I *am* tired. Sick and tired of this job, this endless battle with the brass. They expect me to run this department on a shoestring, and instead of backing me up, instead of giving me all the moral support I need, they sit up there on their salaried butts and think of ways to cut the ground out from under me on a daily basis. And I'm damned sick of it, Sara. I'm sick to death of it."

Siry suddenly grimaced and clutched his left shoulder. "Damn it," he muttered.

"What is it?"

"Pain. Right here at the tip of the shoulder."

"How long have you been having it?"

"Christ, I dunno. Couple of months."

"How bad and how often?"

"Never mind. It's bursitis."

"Whenever you have pain there, at your age, it's cause to see a doctor."

"To hell with doctors. Overpaid quacks."

"You ought to get it checked out."

"Don't nag. We were talking about *you*. I'd like to see you change your attitude. You think you're invulnerable. You're just laughing this business off. But it could happen. They not only could boot you off the force, they could drop a conspiracy charge on you like a bag of hammers."

"Nice image."

"There you go again!"

"Sorry, Cap. It's just that it's hard to take Morrison seriously, let alone Seltzer. They are both so totally clueless. They haven't the slightest idea of what's really going on."

"And you know what's really going on?"

"No, but I have my own fall guy."

Siry's expression softened. "You do?" he asked with genuine interest.

"Yup."

"This guy have a name?"

"Yup. Erwin Strauss. Austrian by birth, former STASI officer. East German secret police and intel. I had some Eurocops fax me his file."

"What's he do?"

"He's been a general utility hit man for the Organizatsiya for over ten years. He's very good. Skilled, intelligent, crafty, and has never been arrested in his life."

"Sounds good. And he's here in New York?"

"For the moment. He did the Bubnov hit, and I think we can make all these weird murder cases stick to him."

"Wonderful," Siry said. "But that doesn't sound like you. Anybody else, I would say, how can we set him up? But you're not usually so cynical. What happened?"

"He's so slimy, he deserves anything he gets. I read his file. He supervised torture. It was his specialty. He's cesspool slime."

"I can show you a hundred guys in Attica who are worse just on paper. I guess you're not really turning cynical after all. Okay, I like him for all this stuff. When can we pick him up?"

"I'm working on it, Cap. I'll let you know."

"Okay, okay." Siry was nodding and looking better. "Yeah. Good." He sat back and continued nodding.

Sara decided this was a good moment to get up and get out. He was still nodding, heaven knew to whom, as she closed the door.

"Good night, Joe."

"Huh? Yeah, good night."

* * *

New York was quiet that evening. A hush pervaded the million-footed city. Baba sat at a small table, laying Tarot in patterns on its top.

Sophia sat in a comfortable chair off to one side. "What do you see, old woman?"

"Death."

"I hate that card. Whose death do you see?"

"A woman's. She is powerful, but she will die."

"That is a good sign for us."

"I see no good at all," Baba said.

"We will avenge Lazlo."

"Is that so important?"

"It is to me. Besides, we cannot run his business with such a potent adversary about."

"Why do you think you can take a man's role?"

"I was the only thing giving him substance. He would never have risen in the ranks if I hadn't pushed him. I grew weary of being the woman behind the man. Now he is gone. I grieve for him, but now I am free. I will stand where he fell and carry on."

"You dream," Baba said, laying another card. "Ah," she added, nodding.

"Oh, play your cards, do your magic. Mr. Strauss is doing the actual work."

"He works with what I give. He has nothing himself."

"Except strength and brains and skill." Sophia snorted. "Nothing, my eye."

"My eye sees the future. It is not good to summon demons to do one's bidding. They will turn. They always do. They are smarter than we. They are dangerous."

"I don't know if I entirely believe in that nonsense. Like Lazlo, I tend to be skeptical."

"It is working beyond my wildest dreams," Baba said. "If I had known, I could have been queen of Romania, and Hungary, and perhaps all the Russias. Had I known. Had I the courage. But I am only a poor old woman. I do not really think it is my magic. It is the witch woman's."

"Oh, hush. How can that be? The witch woman casts an evil spell on herself?"

"I do not understand the nature of her familiar. But he is wily, and perhaps treacherous. Succubi are that way."

"And this succubus is really doing the magic. Against her?"

"That is the way I see it. As I say, I do not completely understand, but I see."

"Ridiculous. Mr. Strauss is a skilled magician himself."

"Oh, he knows more than he can actually do. He is evil incarnate himself, but he has limitations."

Sophia looked at her grandmother-in-law suspiciously. "Sometimes you surprise me. Most of the time you play the idiot. But you are shrewd in your way."

"That is the way I choose to play my cards," the old woman said.

Sara got home late and didn't know what to do. She wanted to worry about her predicament, feeling somehow obliged. It was serious enough. A man had been assigned the task of killing her, and his past history tended to speak highly of his qualifications for that job. He was a professional and had a track record of fulfilling his contracts.

For some reason, though, she could not muster an overall sense of urgency, the sense of danger and alarm most people would feel with a price on their head. She was more worried about not being worried than she was . . . well, whatever.

There was a sense of improvisation hanging over this entire affair, and she had to get to the bottom of it. Someone was behind it. She could not take werewolves seriously. Or Mah Jongg dragons. The werewolf had not taken himself seriously, at times.

The city of the temple, though, for some strange reason, she took as real. Which was all the more strange, because it struck her as the most improbable of the recent apparitions. Nevertheless, those surpassingly strange beings seemed in deadly earnest.

Why on earth would they want her as a goddess? They weren't human. Wouldn't they require an anthropomorphic god from their perspective? Judging from the design of their cities, they were avian. Birds. And their resident (if you could use the term) god was definitely of the same genus. Why would they want an alien creature, which she certainly was, for a goddess? Not a lot of sense there.

Then again, humans have had human gods and non-human gods. Maybe the bird worshipers wanted to trade theirs in on a new model. She wondered about the consequences of such blasphemy. Would not the resident god be. . . . miffed?

Rather miffed, one should think. Then again, who says this god is a jealous god? Don't model your theology after the earthly kind.

The Witchblade began to pulsate.

Ah-hah. And why would that be? Suddenly her hearing became more acute. The door seemed to vibrate with echoes from the hallway, echoes of heavy footsteps. The sounds came from the stairwell, growing louder and nearer.

She got out her .38 special and looked it over, pondering. She had a suspicion, and if it proved accurate, the gun would do her no good. Joe had warned an indictment was imminent. What she needed was a good lawyer, not a representative of the firm of Smith & Wesson. She put the gun back in the drawer of the nightstand.

A bothersome thought occurred. Hell, she'd spend the night at the Tombs, and they'd take the bracelet. She had never thought of that. Damn it, that could not happen. And in jail, without the Blade she would become a fish in a barrel. Through his mob connections, Strauss could reach his tentacles into the Tombs like a giant squid probing a sunken cathedral.

How many disgruntled former informants would there be in the Tombs, more than ready to act out their revenge fantasies by whacking a supposed dirty cop? Plenty. Sure, she'd be segregated, in the women's wing, and probably in special custody reserved for dirty cops. But who knew what guards were on the Organizatsiya payroll?

What could she do? Nothing. Her taking a powder would not only reflect badly on Joe Siry; it could cost him his job and retirement.

An authoritative rap sounded on the door. Sara opened it.

"Detective Pezzini?"

"Yes?"

A strange-looking man flashed a badge at her. He was flanked by four equally odd-looking ducks.

"Who the hell are you?" She didn't see any reason to be civil. "Never seen you before. What precinct do you work out of?"

"We have a warrant for your arrest."

"That so? What charge, exactly?"

"Criminal conspiracy." He fluttered a blue-slipped paper at her.

"So they didn't go for the RICO rap? Okay, come in."
They followed her into the apartment.

"We also have a search warrant," the leader said.

Sara narrowed her eyes. "What's your name and rank? I'd like to know who's commanding this detail."

"Detective Smith," the man said.

"Okay . . . Smith."

"You have the right to remain silent," Smith recited. "Anything you say can and will be used against you. You have the right to an attorney. If you cannot afford an attorney, one will be provided to you free of charge. Do you understand these rights?"

"I don't understand why you're telling me you have a search warrant, when you don't need one on a bust. You can trash this apartment if you want to. You're telling me the DA doesn't know this?"

Smith's eyes suddenly grew . . . strange. Everything was simply wrong. All these jamooks had an odd look. The Witchblade's pulsing was verging on the painful. Sara took a few steps back from "Smith."

"Sara Pezzini . . ." the creature named Smith began.

"You're not from New York, are you?"

Smith shook his head. "No, Sara Pezzini. We want you to come with us."

"Come where?"

"To our world. Please accompany us. We will escort you."

She turned and took them all in. They were simply standing around as if not knowing what to do. Perhaps the others could not even talk.

"Please do come. We invite you."

"Who are you?"

"We are the Order of the Raven," Smith said simply.

"And what is that?"

"It is hard to explain."

"Okay, Order of the Raven. What the hell do you want?"

"We need you to reign over us, as our deity. You and the symbiotic entity." He pointed to her wrist.

"The symbiotic entity?" Sara held out her right wrist. "This bracelet?"

"Yes. You are one thing, it is another. Together, you are yet a third. A godhead."

"And you want me as your . . . deity?"

"Yes. We desire it with every fiber of our collective being. Will you come?"

"No. You come from a funny kind of place."

"Funny?"

"Yeah. Most places, you go to them. Your world is the kind of place that comes to you. I've been there. It's not my kind of town. No offense."

"Ah," Smith said with deep regret. Somehow he looked crestfallen, for all that his mask-face had not changed one iota.

Sara did not understand how that could be, but set the issue aside for the moment. "What I want to know is, why? Why do you want me as a goddess?"

"Relations with our present god have become strained beyond all possibility of repair."

"I see. I don't understand, though."

"Again, it is not easy to cast into terms which you could understand in your present state of consciousness."

"No doubt. How can I get a change of consciousness?"

"We believe you will come to understand through the altered states afforded you by virtue of your symbiosis."

"I don't think of it as a symbiosis," Sara told him. "I

am an independent, self-contained individual. I do feel a kind of obligation to this thing on my wrist. It's chosen me for a role in a drama that's been going on for a long time. Exactly what that drama is all about, I really don't know. I'm still struggling to understand. But that is the extent of my relationship with it."

"We are not entirely knowledgeable of some things. We do not completely understand the entity you wear on your person, and your own nature is mostly a mystery to us. Forgive our presumption in posing some hypotheses."

"I forgive you. I'm going to confess that I haven't the foggiest notion of what you people are all about. And frankly, again no offense, I wish you'd leave me the hell alone."

"If that is your wish, we cannot refuse. However, we cannot let the issue rest. Not yet. Our humblest apologies."

"Smith" bowed deeply, turned and walked out of the apartment. Single file, his buddies followed.

The door closed softly.

"Sheesh," Sara said, shaking her head.

After microwaving a frozen dinner and eating it while watching TV, she went to bed and dreamed about dark skies full of birds, and creepy guys with masks all running about below, getting crapped on and liking it.

Next morning, she stopped into her favorite coffee shop and bought a hot mocha latte with whipped cream. A square of cinnamon crumb cake took her fancy, and she got that, too. Then, sitting at a table eating it, she remembered that a contract was out on her life, and that she should get her butt out of public view, pronto. So she gathered up the cake on a paper napkin and, coffee in the other hand, walked to the station. Some patrolman was kind enough to open the door, but he let it go prematurely. She got bumped in the rear and got her hand scalded. She dribbled coffee and crumbs all the way to her desk.

"Sara, I've got something to tell you," Jake said behind her back.

"What . . . oh, damn. Jake, did you know you had a way of sneaking up on people?"

Jake looked down at the crumb cake, now on the dirty station floor. "Oops. Sorry."

"Rats, that was good, too. Okay, what is it now?"

"Uh . . . Jeez, Sara, I don't know how to tell you this . . ."

"Tell me. It was a bad night and it's been a bad morning so far. Nothing you could say could put me in a worse mood."

"Wanna bet?"

"No. What is it?"

"You're under arrest."

TWENTY-ONE

The worst thing about a stay in the Tombs is the smell, a multi-layered phenomenon. On top of everything sits the fumes of a strong disinfectant, capstone to a wall of odor that permeates the place. The stink of all manner of body effluent, from armpits to excrement, lives in the mid-levels. And bottoming all of it, on the floors and along the walls and baseboards, in drains and pipes, amongst the dust bunnies beneath the bunks and in the musty stuffing of mattresses, dwells the dank smell of mold, mildew, and fungus of every variety, a century in the growing.

The women's wing was a little better than the men's, but not much. Sara had spent all day here. It was evening now, and there was nothing to do but lie in the bunk. At least the sheets were clean. Well, as clean as they could get. The fabric looked to have been woven sometime in the 1950s. It was threadbare and rife with holes. At least the blanket didn't smell. Not much, anyway.

She hadn't been alone. Joe Siry had come and gone, promising to pull every string he could to get her special treatment. She did not tell him not to. No way. She needed every break she could get. One good thing, she had no cell mates. If there had been another cop in jail at the time, maybe. She was alone in the cell, though there were two other cots.

One toilet, the usual stainless steel affair, open to public view.

Charming.

Jake McCarthy had come and gone. He was upset and worried, but tried to cover up with smarmy cheer. She'd beat the rap. No problem. They'd get a good lawyer. He knew a woman who was a great trial performer. She'd get Sara off, if she didn't get the case dismissed at the pretrial hearing.

Sure, Jake. Sara had gone along, surfing on Jake's wave of Pollyanna optimism. But as she had told Joe, she needed a fall guy. And the guy she had in mind was rather difficult to pin a conspiracy charge on. And just how does one go about making a measly state charge stick to a genuine international man of mystery?

The lights went out. It must be ten o'clock. Ten o'clock. That means up at six. Ye gods.

No, don't say "gods," please.

She lay still until her eyes got used to the dark. When forms appeared in the shadows, she rolled over on her left side, plumped the thin pillow, and tried to get some rest.

She was just about to doze off when she caught movement in her field of vision. Something skittered through the cell door and disappeared under her cot.

She jumped up. She hadn't got a good look at it. Spider, roach, mouse, rat, something like that. One of those critters. Well, jails had 'em in abundance. She got on her knees and peered under the bunk. She couldn't see a thing. No matter. If it had been a spider, it probably wasn't poisonous. A mouse she could live with. A rat? It hadn't looked big enough. Likely it had been an oversized roach. So what.

She got back on the cot and stretched out.

Drifting out of sleep, she became aware of something nibbling at her right hand. She rolled out of the cot, hit the floor, rolled again, and brought her hand up to catch the light that had just come on out in the corridor.

The Witchblade was hugging her wrist, throbbing urgently. *This* was what she had seen scurrying under her cot?

"Sometimes you really blow my mind, kiddo," she told it as she picked herself up and got back on the cot. "Glad to see you, though."

A guard appeared at the cell door and fumbled with keys. Sara sat up and looked at him.

"What's up?" she asked, squinting at the light.

"You're being transferred," he replied. He was a big man with a short haircut. He looked like a typical turnkey.

"Funny, nobody told me," she said, wondering what the Blade was warning about. And then the obvious answer occurred to her.

"There's probably a good reason," the guard said pleasantly. "Let's go. Your new cell is in another cell block. Guess they want to keep moving you around for safety's sake."

"Do we need the cuffs?" Sara asked, wanting to avoid his seeing the bracelet. She shouldn't have it.

"Don't see why," he said amiably. "I don't think you're going to try anything, Detective Pezzini. You probably want to get this thing cleared up real fast. Have a good lawyer?"

"Haven't met her yet. Will tomorrow at the arraignment."

"Well, good luck. Hey, I'm on your side. We cops have to stick together."

"Yeah, sure."

"Let me get that," the guard said, applying a key to the cell block door.

"You kinda have to," Sara said. "Don't have my key on me."

The guard laughed and let her through the door.

It was a long way, though door after door. Eventually Sara found herself walking through empty corridors that didn't look like cell blocks at all.

"Where the hell are we going?" Sara asked, turning her head.

The so-called guard was aiming a silenced pistol at her.

In the quiet of the night, the shot made a lot of noise, a sharp whack that echoed off cold concrete.

The Witchblade jumped up to ward off the slug, which went whizzing off at an angle and thunked into the wall a few feet down the hallway.

"What the hell?" the bogus guard said in shock. His eyes widened at the sight of Sara's curlicue gauntlet shapeshifting on her arm. He aimed and fired again.

Same result.

Sara grabbed the gun off him and pocketed it. "Tell Strauss he'll have to come up with better stuff," she told him.

The guy was backing off, eyes as round as manhole covers. "What the hell is that? What the hell *are* you?"

"Oh, Strauss didn't say? Good. You'll never know. Give you something to think about in your old age. If you reach it. By the way, what's your name?"

Nonplused, the phony guard could only answer, "Sam."

"Say good night, Sam."

"Good night."

She sent a simple bolt of kinetic energy at his jaw. Just a tap. He flew about six feet and ended up a sprawl on the blue-painted floor.

She found an emergency box, broke the glass, pulled the cord, and waited for the real guards to show up.

After Sara's arraignment, at which she pleaded not guilty to a charge of criminal conspiracy to commit murder, Joe Siry bailed her out, putting his own house up as security for the bond. Sara emptied her meager savings account and paid Joe what she could, and signed a promissory note for the rest. She had to borrow from the police credit union for legal expenses.

Her lawyer, Cathy Greenwood, was a small woman with an attractive, elfin face. She looked young, very young, but said she was 35 years old. She just had that kind of face. Sara was not reassured.

Siry was forced to suspend her without pay. He had no choice, of course. She could not continue to work while under indictment for a felony. Full back pay would be awarded if she beat the rap. To Sara, though, pay wasn't an issue. It meant she could not do any further investigating on her own. Her badge would be temporarily inactive. She instructed Cathy to ask if she could be kept on active status with the police department.

"We can't have her investigating her own crimes," Morrison, the assistant DA, said.

"Alleged crimes," Cathy Greenwood corrected.

"Of course, alleged crimes."

"Nevertheless, you'd better plead your client. We have more than enough to bind her over for trial."

"We'll see," Cathy said. "Frankly, I don't think you even have a case. I just might mount a defense at the hearing."

"Be a mistake," Morrison said. "If you have a defense, you'll want to save it for the trial. Don't want to tip your hand."

"I'm always suspicious," Cathy said, "when the prosecutor starts giving me courtroom advice. Usually means he doesn't have anything to back up his case."

"We have forensic evidence, we have witnesses, we have the defendant's own statements and official reports."

The DA was leaning forward in his chair, looking uncomfortable. "We wouldn't go to trial if we didn't think we had a case," he said, more to Morrison than anyone else. "Would we?"

"No way, Cap," Morrison said.

"I think what you have are surmises, assumptions, and just plain guesses. My client is a police officer. She's investigating the very crimes you accuse her of committing. Of course you're going to find evidence of her presence at the crime scene. The whole thing is ridiculous. An outrage."

"It's not outrageous to prosecute crime," the interim DA said. "That's our job."

"Absolutely," Morrison agreed, not at all thrilled by the DA's insipidity.

"My client has been attacked in custody. Clearly an assassination attempt. Doesn't that throw doubt on the case?"

"Who knows what mob rules she broke or what toes she stepped on?" Morrison said, his hands out. "I think it tends to bolster our case rather than the reverse. It's clear she has mob affiliations."

"It's also logical to assume that she's a mob target because of her zeal in pursuing organized crime figures."

"That's your interpretation," Morrison countered.

"It will be the jury's interpretation as well," Cathy said.

"We'll see at the trial."

"We won't even get to the hearing. I'm filing a motion for dismissal."

"On what grounds?" the DA asked.

"Lack of evidence. Let's face it, you didn't investigate any other suspects. I wonder what tale the jail hit man has to tell. Who was bribed? How did he get in there? You haven't even offered him immunity.

Morrison said, "We're not obliged to. That's another case entirely. Simply because your client was the intended victim has no bearing on this case."

"I should say it does," Cathy said hotly. "Ridiculous to say it doesn't!"

"Not at all. I think you're making a mistake taking that tack."

"Why so?"

"Well, if you're claiming that the real conspirators are trying to bump off your client, it could be a bid to hush her up in a plea bargain."

Cathy sat back. "Oh," she said quietly. "I see."

"Kind of blindsided you," Morrison said with some satisfaction. "That's exactly what we'll be countering if you bring up the hit attempt."

"But the whole thing rests on appearances," Cathy said lamely.

"Where there's smoke, there's fire," the DA said in hopes of being relevant to the issue at hand.

"True," Morrison acknowledged diplomatically.

Sara was sitting with her long legs crossed, following the exchange with interest.

"You have the semblance of a case," Cathy went on. "But you have no case. It's all appearances."

"Appearances can be deceiving," the DA blurted, then realized he had said the wrong thing. Morrison gave him a sidelong look of irritation.

"Exactly my point," Cathy went on. "My client looks guilty, and lacking any other line of investigation, you target her. She was strictly a target of opportunity, and that's what the jury will think."

"Oh, we're back to the trial again?" Morrison grinned impishly. "Counselor, you'd better plead your client."

Cathy looked at Sara before saying, "What are you offering?"

The DA started to say something, but was preempted by Morrison.

"Murder Two," he said. "Twenty-five to life."

"For which murder?"

"Any of them."

"That's absurd. Sir, weren't you about to say something?'

"Yes, I was," the DA said indignantly. "I was about to offer immunity in exchange for information about the new ethnic mobs." The DA was suddenly all business. "I'm on a crusade," he added, wanting to be helpful.

Morrison was dismayed. "Uh, well, wait a minute . . ."

"I'm the District Attorney."

"Hold it," Cathy said. "Are there two offers on the table? One from the DA and one from the assistant DA?"

"No, there's one offer," the DA said, satisfied to have put his foot down.

"Immunity. Uh, in exchange for reliable information which could lead to a prosecution, which . . . well, which could lead to a conviction."

Cathy was incredulous. "Is the plea bargain going to be contingent on a desired verdict?"

"No, no, not at all," the DA said. "We can offer witness protection, too."

"But that's a federal program," Cathy said.

"We are starting up our own program, funded by . . ."

"It doesn't matter. My client is innocent of any conspiracy charge."

"She's the mistress of a Russian mobster!" Morrison exploded.

"Okay, that's it," Sara said suddenly, getting to her feet. She towered over the DA.

"Uh . . . yes?"

"No plea bargain, no deal, no nothing," Sara said. "There's only so much nonsense I'm going to put up with."

"Counselor," Morrison said, "tell your client she's not helping her case with that attitude."

"Sara, sit down, please. I'm not going to do anything you don't want me to do. Trust me."

"Cathy, I trust you. File your motions, make a defense at the hearing, do anything you have to do, but don't ever consider the possibility that I'll cop a plea to something I didn't do."

"If I had a nickel for every time I've heard that in this

office," Morrison said, shaking his head. "Next day, they bargain."

"There won't be any bargains, not today, not any day," Sara said. "And you won't get a nickel from me, Mr. Morrison."

She executed an about-face and walked out of the office.

Albert the DA was impressed. "Your client has spunk, that I'll say."

"Please," Morrison said.

TWENTY-TWO

To say that Joe Siry's day had been rough would have been an understatement. Sara was out of jail, but had blown the interview with the DA, and Joe had gone to considerable lengths to soften Albert up for some kind of deal. Hell, she could have promised him anything. Information. She had information to trade. Didn't she date that Russian mobster? Well, okay, once, but she could have given them details about him, stuff for their files. Stuff they wanted. Mostly trivial, but Albert would have gone for it.

Promise them anything. That's what he always did. Promise them anything and deliver what you got. Bupkis. Nada. The old bait and switch.

But, no, she had to go and blow it, walk out in a huff. She didn't know you saved that tactic for when they're desperate to make a deal. That's a last-resort ploy. It was a tricky maneuver. He'd pulled it off any number of times in his career.

Sara was young and inexperienced. Hot-headed, impulsive. Most young cops were. She was dedicated, for sure. But she had a wild streak. And that . . . weird business she was always into. He still didn't know what to make of all that.

He left the office and walked to his favorite bar, Grogan's, on West 34th Street. It was a nice little place. He knew the owner, Shamus Grogan, an old reprobate who had long lived on the peripheries of what was left of the ancient Irish mobs of New York. He was long in the tooth, Shamus was. In and out of the hospital for the last ten years. He must be in his nineties by now, but he still showed up at his own joint once in a while to have a glass of Guiness.

There now. He, Joe Siry, was an old acquaintance of Shamus Grogan. Did that mean he had "organized crime affliations," for pete's sake? Don't make him laugh. Same thing with Sara. So she took a fancy to some Albanian. Whatever. So what? Didn't mean she was his mistress. Did it?

Well, Joe didn't really know everything about Sara's love life. That was her business. Right? Right.

He walked in the door. The place was empty, but it wasn't even four-thirty yet. He'd knocked off early. Some days, you gotta knock off early.

A man was standing behind the bar, washing glasses. Joe had never seen him before. "You the new bartender?"

He was a thin and wiry guy with long hair. "Yeah, just got hired."

"What happened to Frank?"

"He needed some time off. Family."

"Oh," Joe said. "This your first day, huh?"

"Yes, sir. What can I get you?"

"The usual. Oh, yeah, you don't know my usual. Half and half."

"Yes, sir, coming right up."

"And some peanuts. Shamus always likes peanuts on the bar."

The new man looked at the clock. "I guess I should get them out. Happy hour coming up."

"Happy hour," Joe said to himself. "I'm happy."

"Yeah?" the guy said, not getting the irony.

"As a lark. When I'm here. When I'm drinking with my buddies. Then I'm happy. If only I didn't have to go to work."

"Oh? What do you do?"

"Police."

"Oh, you're Joe Siry?"

"Yeah. My reputation precedes me, I bet."

"Sure. I've heard of you. Just wanted to make sure."

"Wanted to make sure. What do you mean?"

Suddenly, the front door slammed shut.

Joe jerked his head around. Another guy had slammed it. Big guy. With a gun. "Hey, what the hell is going . . . ?"

"Captain Siry?"

Joe whirled on his barstool to find the voice. A slim, well-dressed man had come out from the back. His face was extraordinarily ugly. The man was a well-groomed toad.

Joe scowled. "Who the hell are you?"

The toad bowed. "Permit me. My name is Erwin Strauss."

Merlin was writing a program on one of his many laptop computers when he heard the cops knock. He always knew when cops knocked: a certain sharp, authoritarian rap, as unmistakable as Morse code.

Muttering mild profanities, he went to the door and

peered through the peephole. He saw a pretty face, a familiar one, distorted by the extreme wide-angle lens. It was pretty even with the distortion.

Well, he couldn't very well pretend he wasn't home. That never worked. He opened the door. It was Pezzini and another guy, likely her partner. He looked like someone out of an old beach movie.

"Merlin," Pezzini said. "You are one elusive dude."

"I like it that way. Do come in."

Merlin led them into the living room.

"This a bust?" he asked casually, knowing they would have said so immediately but wanting to set the tone of the visit.

"Did you know you have about two dozen cell phone accounts?" Sara said. "All inactive?"

"Oh, yeah. Never seem to get those cleaned up."

"And none with a real address. How did you manage that?"

Merlin shrugged. "Talent?"

"Wonder how many cloned cell phones we could find if we searched this sty?" the surfer dude said.

"Plenty, but I get the feeling you guys want to know about something else."

"Yes, we do," Sara said. "Your connection with Irons International Investments and Holdings."

"I've worked for them."

"Or for Kenneth Irons personally?"

"Same thing, no?"

"Not quite, but you have been working for him?"

"Right."

"On what?"

"Big computer."

"What kind?"

"Supercomputer. Powerful one. New type."

"What's it for, Merlin?"

"Controlling the economic world."

"You're being quite forthcoming, aren't you?" Sara said, absently kicking debris.

"Got nothing to hide. It models the world economy, taps into data bases, and comes up with strategies for making money. Big project, but pretty simple concept."

"Got anything to do with computer crime?"

"At Irons's level, there's no such thing. If there is, they call it arbitrage."

"I'd be willing to bet that an investigation would determine the crime angle pretty quickly," the beach blanket dude said.

"I'm just a technician," Merlin said hastily.

"Sure," Sara said. "You only work here. There. Where is 'there,' by the way?"

"You mean the computer."

"I don't mean Hoboken."

"They blindfold me."

Sara and the blond guy exchanged looks. The guy said, "That so?"

"Yup."

"So you don't know where this computer is," Sara said.

Merlin looked out the window. "I might."

"What do you mean?"

"Depends on what chips you put on the table, vis-à-vis Yours Truly."

Sara looked at her partner. "Sounds like he wants a deal, Jake."

"Sure does," Jake agreed.

"Let me ask you this," Sara said. "Did you send the e-mail about Joe Siry?"

"Who?" Merlin said.

"My boss."

Merlin did a take. "Your boss? I don't get it."

"The e-mail sent to my on-line address, informing me he'd been kidnapped. Did you send it?"

"No! I don't know your e-mail address. Anyway, I didn't send any e-mail about any kidnapping. Never. Not ever. No way, man."

"Jake, what do you think?"

"I was watching his reactions. I'm willing to buy them as genuine."

Sara said to Merlin, "Does the name Erwin Strauss mean anything to you?"

"Not a damned thing. Hey, I had nothing to do with it. Your boss, for God's sake. We *are* talking about a policeman, here, right?"

"Right. Strauss claimed credit. You see, there's a contract out on my life, and Strauss took it. This a good way to get me in range, at least. The e-mail suggested a sort of exchange. He'll release Siry if I'll meet him on the field of honor, as he put it, for a personal duel. I want to find out where Lieutenant Siry is being held. I've connected Irons with you, and now, if I can connect Irons with Strauss, I can probably find my boss and free him."

"And you think the computer installation is a good place to look?" Merlin asked.

"It's a start," Sara said. "It's secret. That sounds promising."

"Yeah, I can see where you're going," Merlin said. "What's in it for me? Wait, let me put it this way. What's not in it for me?"

"What's not in it?" Jake said airily. "Mucho jail time for whatever we find in this room. This looks like Evidence City for the computer crime squad."

"Ah-hah," Merlin said, with a profound nod. "I think I see where you're going. Uh . . . okay."

"Okay what?"

"I'll take you to the installation."

"I thought you said . . ."

"Ain't no one can keep me from knowing where I'm going in Manhattan. By ear alone, I know exactly where the place is. And I have other ways."

"Yeah?" Sara said.

"I got my mojo working, baby."

"That is so retro," Jake said.

Sara looked out the windshield. This neighborhood was beginning to look familiar.

Driving, Jake was saying, "Merlin your real name?"

"Middle name," Merlin said. "Lloyd Merlin Jones. My mother always wanted a kid named Merlin, but my dad insisted on naming me after my grandfather. I've always preferred Merlin. Suits my nature."

"How long have you been into magic?"

"Since I was a whelp."

"There's been a lot of magic about lately," Sara said. "And you seem to be behind a lot of it."

"Me? But you the witch lady," Merlin said.

Sara looked at him sharply. "What makes you say that?"

"I didn't know who you were up in Connecticut, but when Irons mentioned you, I put two and two together. You're the witch chick I've been hearing about. Witch cop."

"Where have you been hearing it?"

"On the street. You have no idea how much has been out about you. Some wild witch policewoman who kills guys, messes them up."

"My name's out there?"

"No, no. No names. They don't know who you are. But I do, now. It's got to be you. Man, you're scary."

Sara shoved her hands deeper into her jacket pockets. "I've encountered some weird stuff in my career," she said, trying to sound as noncommittal as possible.

"Like that weird stuff up in Connecticut? Oh, by the way, I finally figured out why Yuri got fried."

"Why?"

"His shots scared the thing."

"He saw it? I thought white dragons are invisible in snow."

"You can see white on white, sort of," Merlin said. "Yuri saw something big moving toward him. He shot at it. The dragon freaked out and vomited fire. A nervous reaction, that's all. Like I said, dragons aren't evil in Chinese mythology."

"I don't believe what I'm hearing," Jake said. "You guys saw dragons in Connecticut?"

"We think," Sara said. I didn't see anything at all. I did see the werewolf. Or someone dressed like one. You're sure it wasn't you, Merlin?"

"Are you kidding me?"

"Didn't think so," Sara said. "Okay, it sounds good. We'll put that one down to 'accidental death by dragon.' As if."

"As if?" Merlin said.

"As if you can put that in an official police report," Jake supplied.

"I get the feeling *all* of this is kinda off the record and

221

unofficial," Merlin said. "I mean, you can't write any of this crap in a report. And not get carted off to the nut nursery."

"Remember all the crap in your room, Merlin," Jake said. "Hardly the stuff that dreams are made of. Get my drift?"

"Got it," Merlin said. "Never mind. Turn into this alley here."

"Is this the place?" Sara asked.

"Near. You should park here. It's walkable."

Merlin sprang the door and jumped out of the car. Sara and Jake were half expecting him to make a run for it. He moved off a few feet, but didn't bolt. He wasn't the type.

"Hope he doesn't get an inkling just how unofficial this is," Jake said.

"Maybe illegal, too, Jake, you don't have to do this. You could get into trouble."

"We get Joe back quick, we don't have a problem," Jake said.

"Let's do it."

They got out of the car and followed Merlin. Sara realized that she was heading east into a neighborhood that she usually entered by a westerly route.

The ramshackle machine shop that was Kool Whip's studio took shape in the gathering fall evening darkness.

Sara said, "You knew Kool Whip."

Merlin stopped in his tracks. He turned slowly. "Uh . . . Charlie Bromley? I knew him. Why?"

"Did you tell Charlie Bromley about any of this witch woman stuff?"

"Yeah. We were talking just recently. Look . . . I had

nothing to do with his death. In fact . . . wasn't it you who tried to arrest him?"

"Tried to *question* him, about the murder of Smokey Drexel."

"Uh-huh," Merlin said, his voice small. He took a deep breath. "Anyway, that's where Whip had his studio. But that's not where the computer installation is. It's under that building."

"The one across?"

"Yeah. That's how I knew this place. I suggested it to Mr. Irons. He bought the whole block. By the way, how were you planning to get in? There's security."

"We have a search warrant," Sara lied.

"Nobody to serve it on. No guards. But there's pretty good electronic security."

"Why no live guards?"

"Security risk themselves, I guess," Merlin said. "Irons wants as few people as possible to know this facility exists. Why he hid it here."

"Then there's no way we can get in?"

"Didn't say that. Follow me."

CHAPTER

TWENTY-THREE

Merlin led the way through a battered door and down a stairwell. At its bottom was a steel door.

"The first layer of security. Keeps the riffraff out. This one's easy."

Merlin took a small tool kit out of his back pocket, extracted a screwdriver from it, went to one knee, and spent only a few seconds picking the conventional-looking lock before standing up and opening the door.

Merlin directed his guests through to a short corridor, at the end of which stood another, more formidable door. It had a lock with a security code keyboard.

Merlin punched a four-digit number, then grasped the door's handle and pulled. Once through, the trio walked another corridor to an imposing vault door that rivaled the best of some big banks.

"Now we have to use high tech," Merlin said. He took out another screwdriver and went to work on some screws in a small panel.

"You seem to have done this before," Sara commented.

"Yeah. Once I figured out the location, I came here

on my own to play with the computer. It's the biggest toy a boy ever had. And I had loads of fun defeating the security."

"Have your fun."

Merlin attached leads from computer to panel and watched patterns dance on the tiny screen. "Won't be a sec," he said cheerily.

"No alarms?" Jake asked.

"I am disarming them as we speak, Detective, sir," Merlin said. "However, there's a camera in the room, and it's always on. We can knock it out, of course. But the video goes to a private security company, and you know how efficient and dedicated the average private security employee is. Armed guards could come storming through the door within ten minutes. Or they could be out to lunch."

"Any way of knowing if there's anybody in there?" Sara asked.

"Not really," Merlin said. "Be prepared to storm in with guns drawn, or do whatever cop thing you guys do."

"Ready to do the cop thing?" Jake asked his partner.

Sara drew her revolver. "Let's do it."

"Uh, I didn't mean right this minute," Merlin said. "Sorry."

With a sharp hiss, the door slid to the left and disappeared into the concrete wall. The portal gave onto yet another corridor and yet another door, this one more massive than all previous.

"What was Irons thinking, nuclear attack?" Jake asked in amazement.

It took a good fifteen minutes for Merlin to open what proved to be the final door to the facility. It opened onto the multi-sided computer control room.

It was deserted. The computer contentedly hummed and flashed in solitude.

"Manny!" Merlin greeted his toy.

"Why do you call it that?" Sara asked.

"It has a dumb name: Macro-Economic Modeling and Simulation Array. MEMSA. That's junk, so I call it Manny. Let me show you how it works."

"We don't have time," Sara said, who had been immensely disappointed at the sight of a deserted facility. Perhaps Strauss and Irons were not connected. That meant a dead end and no further leads.

"We can use the computer's remote viewing function."

Sara stopped her pacing and turned. So did Jake.

"What did you say?"

"Remote viewing. Manny is psychic. I just discovered it recently. One of the reasons I've been visiting on the sly."

"A psychic computer."

Merlin had taken his place at the workstation. "Yeah. It's very cool. It's magic, guys. Manny's not only sentient, he's an adept. He got hold of my magic CD, and I don't really know what happened, but he absorbed it some way. I don't understand how he got it. It may have been when I brought my laptop in for an upload. Must have left the CD on the drive, 'cause Manny got hold of it and copied it. When I saw it on a weird directory, I knew what had happened. This is the world's first magic computer, dudes. You would not believe what it can do."

"Or what it's been doing all along, maybe," Sara said. "This is becoming clearer and clearer."

"Yeah? You mean the dragons and stuff? Maybe, maybe. I've been thinking about that. It's maybe been doing some conjuring."

"No maybe about it," Sara said.

"I guess you're right. All the weird stuff. The monsters."

"You summoned them, Merlin."

Merlin turned on his seat and searched Sara's face for some clue that she had meant it only as a possibility. But his expression betrayed the guilt he felt.

"Shit," Merlin said, turning back to the screen. "I'm a murderer."

"I don't really think so," Sara said. "You said you only meant to cause bad luck."

"I meant for people to stop bothering me. People have always bothered me. I don't want to get into the 'I was beat up as a kid' nerd story, but it's true. I just wanted to get back at people. I didn't mean to kill them. It just happened."

"What did you have against Charlie Bromley?"

"Huh? Same thing I had against Smokey Drexel. I put them up when they got evicted, and they stole my favorite canvas, an original, and sold it to get crack money. Both of 'em. They said they'd pay me back, but of course that was bullshit. I put a curse on both of 'em. And they deserved it. But they didn't deserve to die."

Jake said to Sara, "So Smokey was mugged. Did he have anything to get mugged for?"

"Yeah, all the cash I had in the apartment," Merlin said. "They took that, too. That I would have given them. The painting, no."

"When did Manny get hold of the CD?" Sara asked.

"Couple of months ago, maybe. No telling, though. I've been working for Irons off and on for over a year."

"Okay," Sara said. "It's all coming together. But I have pieces that don't even look like part of a puzzle, much

227

less look like they fit. What was this remote viewing thing you mentioned?"

"Manny can get TV pictures from places where's there's no TV camera. I've been doing . . . well, you can imagine the possibilities."

"Can Manny find my boss?"

"You have a picture of him?"

"Huh? No. Jeez, would I be carrying—?"

"No problem. The NYPD computer would."

"You can log onto it?"

"Sure. No prob. Manny can crack any computer, any-where. I developed programs to deal with almost any situation."

Merlin typed something at lightning speed, grabbed the mouse and clicked. He then alternated between key-board and mouse, working swiftly, expertly.

Very soon, an image of Joe Siry appeared on the screen along with vital statistics from his personnel file.

"Amazing," Sara said.

"Now I'll activate the remote viewing program."

"How's that work?"

"I've no idea how it works or why it works. It just works."

"I'll bet Manny knows."

"Yeah. Okay, here he is."

The CRT showed the face of Joe Siry, and this time it was not a photo. This was a live image. Joe was tied to a chair in a bare room. There was no window in the room, and no real clue as to the room's location.

"Utterly amazing," Sara said. "But not really helpful."

"Yeah, I know," Merlin admitted. "But . . . well, it's a crazy idea, but . . ."

"But what?" Jake prodded.

"There's a summoning spell."

"Which is . . . ?"

"A spell to bring something from a remote location to this location. I've never tried it. Kind of afraid to."

Jake looked at Sara. "What do you think?"

"It's worth a try. It would certainly end the hostage crisis. Merlin?"

"Uh, yeah?"

"Do it."

"Right." Merlin went back to typing and mousing. "I gotta put you in as the summoner, since he's connected to you."

"Do anything you have to. Just get him here."

"I will. Just don't be surprised by unexpected side effects."

"I'll try not to be."

Presently, the huge black wedding cake of a computer began to glow with a faint blue aura.

"Whoa," Merlin said, glancing up.

"Something wrong?" Jake asked.

"Never seen that before. Cherenkov radiation!"

"What the hell is that?"

"It's science creeping into magic. Or the other way around. Hold on."

The aura increased in intensity until it became a flaming aurora borealis effect, a diaphanous fabric of multi-colored plasma filling the room. The intensity became enough to blind. Jake and Sara took cover behind some control consoles, but the effect filled every nook and cranny of the installation and every cubic foot of air.

A blinding blue-white flash exploded in the room, accompanied by a loud pop and a numbing concussion.

When the glow had dissipated and the air was clear

again, Sara stumbled out from cover, trying to make her eyes focus. First she saw Jake and Merlin lying atop each other. They were knocked cold. Then she saw something astonishing.

Joe Siry sat in his chair a few feet in front of the main stack of the computer. He was still tied. He looked around, then looked at Sara. "What in the bloody blue blazes?"

Sara was on him immediately. She cut the ropes with a pocket knife.

"Judas H. Priest," Siry said. "Where did you come from?" He got up, stretched, and looked around. "Where the hell did this place come from?"

"Hard to explain," Sara said. "Never mind. You're back, you're safe. Where was Strauss?"

"I dunno. He might have been in the other room."

"Have any idea where they were holding you?"

"Isn't it here?"

"No. Joe, I said it's hard to explain."

"Well, if it's not here, I don't know. They stuffed me into a trunk."

"The important thing is that we got you back."

"Yeah," Siry said, grabbing his back. "Ouch, damn it. Yeah, thanks."

"What's wrong, Joe?"

"My friggin' arm. Hurts like a bastard."

"Any chest pain?"

"Yeah, some. I'm okay."

"Sit back down. Sit down, Joe."

"Damn," Siry said, clutching his left shoulder. "Going right down my arm. Hurts."

"I'll call 911." Sara took out her cell.

TALONS

"Damn. Damn. God, that smarts. Never thought it would hurt this much."

"Joe, keep calm. Hello? Heart attack, abandoned warehouse . . ." She gave the address.

"Jesus."

"Keep calm. I'm here."

"And so am I," came a voice from behind the stack.

TWENTY-FOUR

Sara turned as a figure came out from behind Manny the computer. It was a large, bearded man in the dress of a past century, somewhere in the Middle Ages. He wore a fur cap and cape, red tunic, black tights, and boots. His eyes were dull black, like soot on a crematorium.

"And who might you be?" Sara asked as the Witch-blade began to transform.

"Vlad Tepys," the man answered. He pronounced the surname *Tepish*.

"So, we finally meet," Sara said. "I've been observing your handiwork for some time."

"I don't know what you mean," Vlad said. "I have been summoned for a killing. You, I think, are the one intended. You can submit now, and I will be merciful. Resist, and I will create a death for you that will linger for an eternity."

"I'll just bet your women can't get enough of you, Vlad," Sara said.

Vald continued walking forward. "You are a beautiful

woman. I've never seen your like. And you have . . .
something . . . what is that thing? Ah." He took another
step. "Ah. I know of that."

"Then you ought to know I will resist," Sara said, "and
that I can provide you with a death that will make one of
your impalings seem like fondling."

Vlad's smile spread across his face like a stain. "You
are tigress. This will be sport for me."

"Let's play," Sara said.

A huge sword with a two-handed haft appeared in
Vlad's left hand, and he advanced swinging it. It made a
swishing sound like an immense scythe.

The Witchblade grew into its blade configuration, a
double-edged shaft of steel that gleamed like a mirror. It
took Vlad's first cut, issuing sparks from where the blades
clashed.

Vlad swung again, and again Sara blocked with her
blade. His cuts were wickedly fast, viciously forceful.
She blocked again and again, and had no time for a
riposte.

But that was not the worst of it. The worst of it was
that the swipes became ever more forceful, the momen-
tum packing more and more punch, until she came
within a hair's breadth of losing her footing.

Vlad's blade came round and hit hers like a runaway
freight train. She staggered and lurched across the room,
hit the wall and sprawled.

Vlad laughed. "A woman warrior. What a silly thing.
How can you hope to stand up to a man?"

Sara picked herself up and looked around. The wall
seemed to have receded. The room seemed bigger now.
Lots bigger, but she had little time to notice.

Vlad came at her. She backed off, having the space now.

Vlad swung. She blocked the blow and a stinging sensation went up her arm like a bolt of electricity.

"Ah, you hurt," Vlad said with satisfaction. "It feels like fire in the arm, eh? Like your hand is on fire. It will hurt more. I will defeat you, little woman, and I will make you feel pain. I will gut you from gills to gullet and relish your screams. Then I will take your soul to Hell with me."

Sara suddenly dropped to her knees and swiped at his shanks. The move forced him into an awkward position, which Sara capitalized on immediately with a thrust at his midsection. He barely knocked the point of her blade away.

"Ai!" He laughed maniacally. "You make it interesting! Lovely!"

He began swinging again, more forcefully than before. Sara got batted around like a stuffed toy and was beginning to think she did not have a chance when something extraordinary happened.

Vlad's head detached from his body and hit the ground. It bounced twice and came to rest. The eyes were round with incomprehension. And the mouth spoke. "What . . . who . . . ?"

Fire came out from the truncated neck.

The body went to its knees. Behind it stood the figure of Ian Nottingham, hair flowing, dressed in studded leather and black velvet.

"Hello, Sara," he said pleasantly.

"Ian! Where the hell did you come from?"

"I believe you summoned me. No?"

"I guess I did," Sara said.

"Not sure of the circumstances, but here I am. Anything I can help you with?"

As if in answer, Vlad's body rose and charged Ian. The

head shifted its eyes to follow the action as it attacked. Ian backed, off parrying slamming blows that seemed to come from all directions. Even headless, Vlad was as demonic as the flames and smoke issuing from the neck.

Sara rushed to attack from the headless body's rear. She thrust at the spine, wondering whether it would do any good to attack anatomical points. It did not. She buried the Blade squarely in the middle of the back, severing what would have been the spine, if it existed, but the body did not go paraplegic, did not collapse. Flame shot out of the hole she had made in the fur cape.

The mouth on the disembodied face roared, and the body turned around. This stereo-like effect was disconcerting. Sara backed off to take the thing's measure.

Ian took advantage of Vlad's presenting his back and attacked. He had some success backing the apparition toward Sara, who lunged.

Vlad's blade came around fast and blocked, then slashed back at Ian. Sara swung, was blocked, then Ian swung and met the same defense on his side. The sword moved fast enough to snap the air like the end of a whip.

Sara and Ian locked eyes and swung together. Vlad chose to block Ian, letting Sara's sword bite through his right arm, severing it at the elbow. Flame shot from the stump.

The head bellowed its frustration again, but the body did not stop fighting. Left-handed, it hacked and slashed at its two opponents.

The fight ranged across the now-cavernous room, which hardly resembled the computer installation any more. The monstrous, unnatural thing fought furiously until Ian managed to land a solid blow on its left shank. The huge form stumbled and fell.

"Witch woman!"

Sara spun toward the disembodied head.

"Tell me. Do you know what they call me?"

"Other than Vlad? Haven't the slightest."

"I am called Dracula."

"Not without justification," Sara said.

"Do you know what it means?"

"Nope."

"The Dragon."

"Uh . . . okay, if you say so."

The headless body disappeared in a gout of flame.

Something else took shape out of the smoke and fire and fluid electricity of the expanded space. An immense saurian form flapped its wings and roared.

"Ian, thanks awfully much for showing up."

"Ah, I do not think the show is over."

"Not by a long shot. How do you propose we deal with this new thing?"

"I propose we run like hell."

"Good idea. In what direction, might I ask?"

"Around in panicked circles, if nothing else."

"Right."

"By the way, when did this room become a cave? A flaming cave, to boot."

"Don't know. Wasn't paying attention."

The dragon opened its mouth and vomited fire. It hit them like the blast of a tactical nuclear weapon.

When the heat had passed off and the acrid fumes dissipated, Sara and Ian raised their heads and looked. The dragon was advancing toward the lake of fire that occupied the middle of the cavern.

Sara felt her eyebrows, checking to see if they'd been

singed off. He felt her hair. It was still intact, at least not on fire.

"I guess I have to handle this," she said.

"Why don't you go and do that, old girl," Nottingham said.

"I wish we were doing Chinese mythology."

"Say what?"

The dragon glided into the liquid fire like a duck taking to water. Flapping its huge leathery wings, it began swimming across, puking flame in a narrow, directed stream like something out of World War Two combat footage.

Sara used the Witchblade to ward it off. Fire splattered to her left and right, dancing off the black rocks, cascading and spreading, dark smoke rising from it.

When the monster paused to take a breath, Sara sprayed.

Not fire, but foam, thinking she'd continue the scientific motif of the original location. The modern stuff hit the ancient dragon and enveloped it in runny white goo, spewing out with a sound not unlike whipped cream from a can. As it landed on the surface of the lake, a great hissing and bubbling commenced. The fire churned and spat.

Sara continued spewing foam, delivering great quantities of the stuff, mounting in the middle of the lake like a mound of dessert topping. Underneath, the fire reacted violently, sputtering and throwing back huge gouts of the foamy stuff. Splatters hit the shore and doused fires among the rocks.

Ian Nottingham stood on the shore of the lake of fire, astounded beyond words. He thought the sight of the dragon being enveloped a singular sight indeed. He applauded.

Sara finally decided enough was enough. She could see nothing but foam, a mountain of it. All it needed was some nuts and a cherry.

She walked over to where Ian was standing. "See the dragon anywhere?"

"No sign of it from this standpoint."

They watched. The foam was sliding and slopping every which way. Something could have been moving underneath at any number of points. Finally, with a splash of foam and fire, the dragon's head emerged. It swam to shore and lay its long neck along the rocks. It coughed and sputtered and spat white stuff. Then it exhaled, and nothing but blue smoke came out.

"Out of gas," Sara said.

The dragon looked at the two forlornly.

CHAPTER

TWENTY-FIVE

Gradually, the lake of foam and fire began to fade. The rocks turned to smooth flagstone. The floor flattened out, and the dragon and his foam coat receded into mist. Perspectives shifted. The subterranean world was gone.

"Sara, I don't know quite how to put this," Nottingham said, his voice growing faint, "but are you by any chance *growing*?"

Sara, already beyond Nottingham's ken and filling another space and a different time entirely, found herself towering over the polished temple floor.

Reality shifted, and the million-stranded warp and woof of existence twisted into a new thread and wove itself into a new fabric.

Screeeeeeeeee . . .

Sara looked up. The Bird approached, consumed with a jealous anger. Its feet were extended, and its talons gleamed with metal. It was not a natural creature. It was a god, and it was angry.

She was ready for it. She looked down at herself. She was a giant. She was the statue she had seen, the Witchblade, standing atop her inlaid pedestal. But there was no roof to her temple. It was open to an infinite sky.

Sara had never taken flight. She did now. She leapt, and the air took her. She climbed on her immense metal wings, wings that rent the air with their beating.

She found it hard work, but felt exhilarated. She rose higher and higher in a widening spiral, into thinner and thinner air, then banked and soared on an updraft.

It was glorious. The wind was in her face and the earth ... no, not the earth, but the ground ... spread out beneath her like a blanket. Pastures, meadows, forest and field, mountains in the distance. An idyllic land, yet a strange one. She saw the city below, the whole of it. It was a tower-covered island between two rivers, and but that was all it shared with its counterpart in Sara's world. There were no other cities around it. It was a bustling urban island in the middle of rural expanses.

She folded her wings and dove, leveled out, rose on thermal currents, dove again and glided. She got the idea then that her wings were merely symbols, that she did not need actual wings to fly. She acquired the overwhelming sense that she could do anything she wanted.

The strange world got smaller, its horizon curving slightly. The sky darkened to violet and clouds were now scudding at her feet. Yet she could breathe. Or she did not need to breathe.

She decided to glide to a lower altitude, gathering speed in great widening circles. Wind snapped at her hair, sent it flowing behind her. She felt the low temperature of these altitudes but did not feel the cold. The winds were icy but they did not bite. It seemed as though she were born for flight.

She grew greater and greater wings. They spread out

against the curve of sky and space, ethereal and yet substantial at the same time, and they undulated rather than beat, like a display of northern lights against the fall of night, like veils of energy, sparkling multi-colored plasma.

Something came up below, a huge palace complex sitting atop a high mountain, a glory of alabaster colonnades and marble porticos. She swooped and landed on a capacious terrace.

She looked down. The world of the Chorus spread out beneath her. She looked around and knew this to be her intended home, her Olympus.

Screeeeeee . . .

The Bird approached, beating its wings furiously, seething with righteous anger, resentful of the intruder, wanting confrontation. It flexed its talons in anticipation, extending them forward, ready to swoop, to pierce, to clutch and tear. It needed prey and it would have it. It needed something to attack, for violence was at the heart of its being, its nature, its reason for existence.

Diving from the terrace, she obliged.

She headed straight for the god-creature and as she neared she sensed something of its fierce nature. It was petty and avaricious, demanding horrendous sacrifices. It loved the smell of fresh blood, and relished pain and suffering.

It bulked huge against the clouds. She had never realized just how massive the creature was. And it was getting bigger.

She extended the gauntlet and directed a bolt of energy at it.

A sharp report split the sky, and the bird-god tumbled, its wings gone slack and rubbery. She was shocked to see that it did not have much strength, for all its bulk. It was too used to bullying creatures of lower link on the great chain of being, much too used to having its sadistic and arbitrary way. After all it was a god, and few can oppose the gods.

She had no trouble. She banked to the right and watched the Bird recover and begin to climb. She glided, picked an angle of attack, and dove, coming at the creature out of the low sun.

At the last minute the Bird executed a whirling turn and counterattacked, bringing its razor-sharp talons up to slash at her. Her gauntlet swiped at them and sent the huge bird tumbling again.

She waited for it to rise again. It seemed dazed a bit, somewhat disoriented, and disinclined to continue the conflict. But it mustered the strength and shot out toward the horizon, needing time and space to gather its resources.

She did not intend to let it. Beating her wings furiously, she took off after it, pursuing it into an expanse of rarefied, etheric blue. She overtook it and directed bolts of searing energy at the bird-god, ionizing energy that came from the depths of her own resources.

The god screamed its pain. It was a new sensation. If it had ever felt pain before, it had been eons since the event. Yet it kept up its counterattack, its talons clicking as they flexed and tried to grab, tried to sink into human flesh, a kind of flesh they had never tasted. The creature was intrigued by its smell. It was sweet.

But it would not get a sample.

A flash of red fire came out of the sky and grew into an explosion of light and radiance that enveloped all of space. The concussion shook the world below and was of such power that it knocked the Bird's true nature loose, the form that it had been hiding for ages. Its true form, that of a vast scaly beast, amorphous and shifting, ever-changing. The Bird was simply a guise, had been its cover and stability for millions of years.

She watched the thing fall, but not wanting to see its end, for she knew it already, she turned and headed back to the palace.

As she alighted on the terrace, a concussion of light grew on the horizon, followed by a huge volcanic gout of flame. The earth had swallowed the Bird for good. It was banished from the skies forevermore.

She looked down at her transfigured form. The Witch-blade had transformed and was now a glory of silver fili-gree, a cloak of scrollwork and arabesque, flowing from her almost naked body and spreading out from her flanks and behind her.

The gauntlet still covered her right arm, and she brought it up to look at it. Its own nature was changing, and hers with it. Together, they were becoming a third entity, something whose dimensions she was just now be-ginning to grasp. Vistas of new consciousness extended before her, ranges of thought and feeling and sense far beyond those of human ken, intelligence and perception undreamed of. Her sensorium cast its net over her proud new world, from which a great chorale of joy had arisen.

My people, she thought. *My world. A world over which I will reign in glory and in truth, in justice and in mercy.*

Joe ... what had happened to Joe?

My domain, my dominion. I am a goddess, and I will reign forever and ever ...

Hallelujah?

Listen to those voices singing praise. I am a god. I am truth and light. I will rule wisely and with compassion ...

What the hell is going on? The Blade. The Blade . . .

Millions singing my praises. I am a goddess, my dominion is the sky . . .

No!

My worshipers are legion. Millions sing my exploits and will for generations untold . . .

No! What happened to Joe? I want to know. He was sick, he needs me . . .

Forget all your earthly ties. Stay here. This is your home. You belong, you are one with this world.

Shut up! Shut up, damn you . . .

Don't go back to that dreary world. Don't give up all this. Don't give up being a goddess!

I must go back. I must.

No!

Have to. Have to. This is not for me. I am not a goddess. I am a human being.

You're more than that with us.

With us? Who's "us"? Tell me that. Tell me finally who you really are!

You will know. You will have the understanding. You will never understand as long as you stay the creature of clay you were born. You must transform and transfigure, and we can help you. You are great, you are a champion. You must stay here.

No. I must go back. You can't drag me along like this. I am an individual, not some component of a gestalt.

You can be, and you will fulfill your destiny.

No. I must decline the honor. I am going back to the world.

No.

I must.

No, please . . .

* * *

She came out of the skies, down from the cold violet reaches, spiraling, gliding, wings extended to their fullest extent, savoring the last of the sensations of flight, sensations she knew she would never experience again.

She touched a foot on the inlaid pedestal.

The Chorus stood at its base, looking up. If their masks could plead, they would. But the masks were unchanged, as masks always are.

She swept her eyes over them. "Do you really need a goddess? Do you need a god at all?"

They all nodded.

"Well, good luck."

She descended the pedestal's steps. "Farewell, people. It was interesting."

There came a shift in the fabric of reality.

She was climbing down from Manny. At the computer's base stood Ian Nottingham. He gave her a hand to the floor. "Must have been a heady experience."

"You were there?"

"Saw it all on the CRT."

"So you know. You saw."

"I saw. I didn't quite get everything. Don't really know what it was all about. I won't ask where it was. Just how it was."

"It was . . . very interesting," Sara said, looking at her wrist. The Blade was back to its bracelet configuration, and she was in mufti. Suddenly, her memory was jogged. "Joe! Where's Joe?"

"He's conscious. They're working on him."

"Who?"

"The paramedics. You've been gone for quite a while. The cavalry arrived."

"He had a heart attack."

"Looks like, but as I said, he's conscious. They're going to be taking him to the hospital. I really would like to get out of here. Oh, by the way..." Nottingham stepped away, reached behind a console, and dragged out a semiconscious Erwin Strauss. "Know this blighter?"

"Yes. Let me get cuffs on him. Where's Jake?"

"Still out cold. I think he'll be all right. Listen, I'm leaving while the leaving is good. I've discovered a back way out of this place. Emergency exit, it looks like. I'm going to use it, right now."

"Thanks, Ian. See you soon?"

"Are you forgetting the bond between us?"

"No."

"Then what makes you think you've seen the last of me?"

With a Cheshire Cat smile, Nottingham strode away. He stepped behind a wall of instruments, and did not reappear again.

"What in the name of God has been going on here?"

She turned to see Kenneth Irons approaching. He looked completely astounded, and thoroughly irritated to see his installation occupied by intruders.

"We've been playing games on your new computer," Sara said with a wry smile.

EPILOGUE

Siry was still in ICU when Sara had time to visit him. The nurse told her that he was recovering nicely, and outlined what procedures they had done.

"So what did they do when they poked that needle up my thigh?" Joe wanted to know.

"They did an angioplasty on two coronary arteries, and inserted stents."

"What the hell are those?"

"Expandable titanium rings that hold the artery open so that blood can flow through them, you fool." Sara raised an eyebrow. "Didn't they tell you anything?"

"I was so doped up I couldn't understand a thing they were saying. What's it all mean?"

"It means you don't have to have bypass surgery. It means that you can go home in a week and watch your diet, exercise, and live."

"And stop smoking, I guess."

"And stop smoking, you fool."

"Don't talk to your boss like that."

"I will when my boss is a fool."

He sighed. "Okay, I'll stop smoking. Thanks for calling the paramedics."

"You remember anything about the attack?"

"Other than it hurt like hell? No. What the hell did go on? How the hell did you get me away from that Strauss guy?"

Sara glanced at the floor and smiled. "I'll explain it someday. Strauss came in very handy. The DA dropped its case against me and prosecuted him."

A big smile sprang to Siry's face. "So you're in the clear?"

"I'm free as a . . . I'm off the hook," Sara said. "The DA ended up with egg on his face, though."

"What happened?"

"The feds wanted Strauss for questioning, and when they took him off to one of their facilities, he escaped."

"Escaped!"

"He's gone. So the DA ends up with nothing to show for all his trouble."

Joe laughed. When he was done he coughed and gasped, "Poor Albert."

"Poor Morrison," Sara said. She glanced at her watch. "Look, I have to run. Enjoy the flowers."

"Thanks, Sara. You know, there was a lot of weird stuff again."

"Yes, there was."

"Good thing I can't remember any of it. But I want to talk about it someday."

"As I said, someday. See you later, Joe."

On her way out, she thought about what was still bothering her.

What had been the source of the magic? The candidates

were Merlin, Baba, and Manny, and none of them seemed strong enough. Something had spooked Manny, and it was undoubtedly Merlin. But who had spooked Merlin in the first place? Or had he become the magician he wanted to be?

Irons? Was Irons behind it all?

No. Irons was no magician. He was a wannabe.

In the hospital lobby, she stopped and looked at the bracelet on her wrist.

Of course. There was only one source of magic that she knew of. The Witchblade must be unhappy, weary of this mundane world it was stuck in. It wanted something better; it wanted to be a god.

"You sons of bitches," she said. "I hope you had fun."

She left the hospital. As she walked along the streets of the city she loved, she could have sworn she heard a faint, distant giggling.